THE CELL BLOCK PRESENTS...

HOW TO WRITE
URBAN BOOKS
FOR MONEY AND FAME

Published by: THE CELL BLOCK™

THE CELL BLOCK
P.O. Box 1025
Rancho Cordova, CA 95741

Instgram.com/mikeenemigo
Facebook.com/thecellblock.net

Copyright© 2018 Wilberto Belardo AKA King Guru

Cover design by Mike Enemigo

Send comments, reviews, or other business inquiries:
info@thecellblock.net
Visit our website: thecellblock.net

TABLE OF CONTENTS

FOREWORD BY DUTCH

PROLOGUE
This book isn't just about writing urban novels. This is actually the story of how we did it.

INTRODUCTION
You're up against a unique challenge whenever writing urban novels because you only have words to work with.

CHAPTER ONE: BLUEPRINT
The first mistake most novice writers make is they start their book without first creating a blueprint.

CHAPTER TWO: LET'S GET IT CRACKIN'
If you have what it takes then what I'm about to give you will enable you to get started within ten days.

CHAPTER THREE: GEMS FOR YOUR BAG OF TRICKS
Writing an urban novel isn't a goal that you can go after half steppin'.

CHAPTER FOUR: MAKE IT UNIQUE
Allow your plot to become the teacher and let the character be the student.

CHAPTER FIVE: YOU REAP WHAT YOU SOW
You can turn anything you experience into a great story.

CHAPTER SIX: CONTROL YOUR IDEAS
The main objective is to get your readers to open your book and enjoy what they read.

CHAPTER SEVEN: CRAFT
I wasn't the man who invented the rules on this craft, but I can lace you with an outline so you can learn it.

CHAPTER EIGHT: PLOT
The plot isn't just about one thing leading into another, it's about watching the main character grow and learn.

CHAPTER NINE: CHARACTERS

An experienced author can make his readers believe the characters in their stories are real people.

CHAPTER TEN: DIALOGUE
You can try to write an urban novel without dialogue, but it won't work.

CHAPTER ELEVEN: POINT OF VIEW
One of the biggest decisions you'll have to make when writing your urban novel is which point of view to tell your story from.

CHAPTER TWELVE: DESCRIPTION'S
The world you create has to seem real, so real that they can feel it, hear it, see it and taste it.

CHAPTER THIRTEEN: SETTING
Just like lighting candles and turning on slow jams will set the mood for romance, there are also ways to set the mood in your story.

CHAPTER FOURTEEN: PACE
There is a common understanding among writers and their readers that says, if you don't snatch your reader's attention within the first fifty pages, chances are, they're gonna put the book down.

CHAPTER FIFTEEN: VOICE
It's the creation of a vibe that you introduce to your readers that will create a voice in their minds without ever having to pick up a phone and speak to you.

CHAPTER SIXTEEN: THEME
If your goal is to write an urban novel that will imbed itself in the minds of all your readers then you better have a theme.

CHAPTER SEVENTEEN: REVISION
Its okay if your first draft isn't platinum, it's not supposed to be.

CHAPTER EIGHTEEN: CHECK LIST
As long as you pay attention and take heed to my wisdom it should be all good for those of you who are willing to put your all into it.

CHAPTER NINETEEN: BUSINESS
If you ever want to get your work published you have to accomplish one thing: You must finish your project.

CHAPTER TWENTY: REJECTION
Instead of letting a fall make you quit, let that fall make you stronger.

CHAPTER TWENTY-ONE: SELF PUBLISHING
If you really believe in yourself then you gotta do you!

A REALLY SIMPLE WAY TO GET RICH!

There is one simple way to get rich. From day one, you could have over one million dollars in less than a year.

CONCLUSION

In this game, just like all the others, it's all about your grind! Never give up! Never take NO for an answer!

8 URBAN FICTION AUTHORS WHO OVERCAME PRISON AND FORGED LUCRATIVE CAREERS

DUTCH INTERVIEW

WAHIDA CLARK INTERVIEW

URBAN PUNCTUATION GUIDE

A WORD FROM MIKE ENEMIGO

URBAN WRITER'S RESOURCES

SNEAK PEAKS

FOREWORD

Everybody has a story to tell. The question is; can you tell it? Life imitates art, but it takes a creative mind to bring art to life.

I've been writing since I was 12 years old. I've crafted Street classics like *Dutch 1-3, Dynasty 1-3*, and *Above the Law*. These are among the most popular and successful Street-Lit books ever written. They've earned me a bunch of money, and I've done it all from my prison cell – where you likely sit now, reading this book. But having the desire to write and an idea for a story are only the first steps of the process. There are crafting laws that must be followed; ingredients a Street classic must contain! And this secret-sauce recipe has largely remained a closely-guarded secret – until now. Mike Enemigo's book with King Guru will give you the game you need on crafting a classic story, such as the art of character arc, dialog, building tension and drama, and other necessary elements. Yeah; you hold in your hands a never-before revealed blueprint I and other incarcerated Street Lit Kings and Queens have used.

I consider Mike a friend and a colleague. It is an honor to write this Foreword, especially since I know this book is going to help you, the next generation of Street-Lit superstars, learn everything you need to know about writing urban books, so you, too, can write Street classics, cement your legacy among the greats, and make a whole bunch of fuckin' money doin' it. Now pay close attention and hustle hard!

Kwame "Dutch" Teague
– Legendary Street-Lit Author

PROLOGUE

Welcome to another production by The Cell Block (TCB). In traditional TCB fashion I'ma get straight to the point. This book is about writing and publishing books. Urban novels, or crime novels, to be exact. The bulk of it is based on cultivating craft, then there's the business aspect, as well as all the resources you can utilize to manifest your goals and aspirations. And though I'm doing this from a prison cell, as are all the TCB authors, this manual is for writing urban novels from both prisons, and the hood.

Ideally, I would like those of you reading this book to already be familiar with not only my writings, but the whole TCB line-up. The reason I feel this way is because Mike Enemigo has taken several years to accumulate as well as cultivate a team of dedicated gamed-up intellectuals who know how to express realism on paper from the inside of our prison cells. If you've already experienced one of our books then you've most likely tested our methods and have eaten off at least one of our tactics. In other words, if this isn't your first TCB feature, you're already part of a secret society of convicts across this nation who refuse to let these prison walls stifle your intellectual prowess.

This book isn't just about writing urban novels. This is actually the story of how we did it. Don't get me wrong, Mike Enemigo is the CEO of TCB. All bullshit to the side, this company came from his vision. This is his brainchild. However, as an individual on the line-up with an unlimited book contract, I can attest that we've all put in countless hours, days, weeks, months, and even years into the products that are circulating throughout the prison system. All of us are real niggaz who've shot people, sold drugs, and gang banged on the streets; and all of us have stabbed people, sold drugs, and gang banged in prison. So, the content we do put out is from reputable convicts and street niggaz.

I'm actually surprised we have pulled off as much as we have. Every time one of us submits a manuscript there's a meeting that follows where the sole subject matter is whether or not Mike should risk putting TCB resources to publish and market a book that "they" may blackball. Not only that, but the risk is always there that one day we'll either be placed on a federal watch list or banned from publishing period. Nevertheless, after all our input is considered and the work passes the criteria mandated for a TCB production, Mike and the TCB staff bust moves and get the heat to y'all.

For those of y'all who are reading one of our books for the very first time, let me give you a quick history lesson. Mike is from the Eastside of Sacramento. Before he fell he was actually in the studio putting together an album. He was also out there getting money in the streets to pay for studio time. All the details are in his *Conspiracy Theory* book. Well, he ended up catching a case for a murder/robbery and caught a life sentence.

Throughout the struggles he never gave up his goals and aspirations for gettin money in the industry. So, blood hit a yard and got himself some shit to make a home-made music studio in his prison cell. Yeah, I'm not giving you all the details because there's really not enough room for it, and Mike Enemigo already gave you the game in his book *Thee Enemy of the State*. So, bruh really rewired some shit and sound-proofed his cell to make a studio. He even moved X-Raided, another Sacramento rapper, into his cell to collaborate with. That is, until he and one of his drillers had to smack X-Ratted for playing with the game. For that story, read *X-POSED!*

After putting hundreds of songs together, sending 'em to the streets to get mastered, he hit a wall. Penetrating the rap game from a prison cell is too hard without the proper funding and industry support. So, blood had to rethink the whole process, and that's where he came up with TCB. He wrote his first book and some money started trickling in. Then he took that money and put on Armando Ibarra and Cascious Green. All this happened before me and him crossed paths, and there have been some financial stumbles and falls. However, you must consider the location we're at. Mike has a life sentence; he's been in prison since 1999, he's been housed on a level 4 yard for over two decades. That said, The Cell Block is now a company making enough money to feed everyone with a contract as well as our families.

While all this was happening, I was bouncing around from state to state, getting extradited back and forth between Florida and Tennessee. I ain't gonna lie, my time hasn't always been on this high-end luxury status that it's on now. Yeah, I had money on the streets, but I've been broke before, too. I know what it's like not to have anyone to call, not to go to the store, not to get mail... But things aren't like that now. Now I'm penitentiary rich! We all are. Listen, I go max draw every month. In California we're allowed to spend $220 a month. If you owe restitution, every $100 you get sent in, they (CDCR) take 55% from it. Well, I owed $15,000 in restitution when I first got sentenced, but I'm down to about 4 racks, and I've still been spending the whole $220 every month.

I've got a 7" tablet with every video game we can order. I've got over 150 30-second videos of my bitches, family and friends. Music? Shit, my playlist is impeccable; over 700 songs. I've got the touchscreen 15" flat screen with a radio and CD player. I've got 4 pair of shoes, all of 'em Jordans. If you got access to the internet you can see for yourself how I'm stuntin' on Facebook. So, yes, I've had several cell phones. Right now, my left wrist is sportin' the same Cartier I was wearing on the street.

I'm not gonna go into all the different bills I've been paying for my baby mammas, but I will say this: My kids are well taken care of. Seriously, though, not all my money comes from my royalty checks. And, no, not even all that money can be attributed to all my in-prison hustles. Outside support in the form of a couple ride or die chicks are the real foundation. B.U.T. (Born Universal Truth), the T.R.U.T.H. is this book shit is what put all of it into play for me.

When I sent my manuscript in from the streets, my book *Underworld Zilla* was already out, and I was pushing it on social media. The energy I received from that was cool.

So, when I fell again and the *How to Hustle and Win: Sex, Money, Murder Edition* dropped, it attracted enough attention that it helped secure a fan club of sorts.

Oh yeah, y'all, you will get a fan club out of getting your book published. It's not only gonna be from females who dig real niggaz in prison. See, once you start doing shit that produces things that people can see and hold in their hands (a book), you'll meet people who will want to help you since you've been helping yourself.

To sum it all up, this book game is real. We've been fuckin' wit' it, and the money is coming fast. If you plan on writing urban novels, you gotta get your game tight. Real talk, you need to have at least 2 aspects of your life mastered, and the first one is the craft of writing. You gotta know how to write. That's what this book is all about. The second thing you have to have is real life experience with the streets. In this life, people are trained to sniff out fake people. When you're writing a book, you're actually opening your mind to the rest of the world. And the world you're expressing yourself to is a world of killers, hustlers, con artist, and pimps; the "worst of the worst." These are the people I write for. These people won't waste their time or money if they detect a hint of suckerism in your work.

One of my main pet-peeves about people who aspire to write urban novels is that most people in prison think they can just sit down and spit out a book whenever they feel like it. It's not that easy, y'all. People actually go to school for this shit. But after reading this book, you'll be good. This book will give you everything (and I mean everything) you need to write a book.

Trust me, you'll see what I'm talking about once you get deeper into this work.

Proper Education Always Corrects Errors!

INTRODUCTION

What is an Urban Novel?

An urban novel is a fictional story based on the lives of individuals living throughout the inner cities of America. Some stories are based on real life events, yet the genre is centered on fiction.

And what is fiction? Fiction is a made-up story. Therefore, an urban novel is a made-up story about people living in the ghetto.

You're up against a unique challenge whenever writing urban novels because you only have words to work with. There are no pictures, sound boards, or movie producers with computer generated special effects. Everything is done with letters we put together to create words which we then put together to create sentences. When done correctly these words will enter the imagination of the reader transforming them into an alternative reality.

Most people enjoy reading urban novels because they crave entertainment. For others it's a way for them to get away from their everyday lives. A well-written story will satisfy both of those needs extremely well. Every urban novel ultimately requires its words to intermingle with the reader's mind in order to take them into a different place and time; giving them a chance to experience life through a sort of looking glass.

If you have the skills to make this happen you will have a bright future in the literary world.

The first step in writing an urban novel is having the desire to do so. Since you've opened this book it's obvious that you have the hunger to learn. That's a good sign; it's a beginning.

I started writing books while I was in prison. Needless to say, I had a lot of time on my hands. However, what I failed to realize in the beginning was that time isn't the only precursor to writing a good story. It takes a certain set of skills to write a good, entertaining urban novel. In my mind, since I knew how to read and write – the rest would fall into place. But what I soon found out was that writing a book was nowhere near as easy as it sounds.

During the first stage of my development, I was so hyped about writing a book I would tell everyone and anyone who would listen about my plans and ideas. That's when I started to see that I wasn't the only person in my cipher who had ideas for a book. Almost everyone you talk to has an idea for a manuscript; and most of them think they can do it whenever they feel like it.

Well, I'm here to tell you that not anyone can sit down and hash out a good urban novel without the proper training in craft. Writing is a craft that takes practice and skill. That's why I decided to write this book in the first place, so I can pass on the skills that it takes to write a bestselling urban novel. I can guarantee that once you finish reading this book you will have a newfound respect for story writing. You will even start looking at other people's work in a different light because you will finally have the knowledge of how the story you are reading was really created. In this book I am giving you tricks of the trade – Jewels of the Game, if you will – that in the past you may have never recognized and had taken for granted. Therefore, it is inevitable that this book is going to make you into a better writer than you are right now.

BASING YOUR STORY ON REAL LIFE DOESN'T ALWAYS WORK

It's not a secret that the best urban novel authors have some sort of tie to the streets. We've really carried pistols, sold dope and were active in the streets at one point or another. Nevertheless, just because you've actually lived an exciting, glamorous life doesn't mean it will come out as a thrilling story when you go to put it down on paper. Right off the top of my head I can give you five specific reasons as to why writing about real life can quickly become a problem:

1. Most people allow the real situation to drive the plot of the story. This stops them from exploring other alternatives that might make the story more interesting.

2. Whenever someone personally knows the characters, they are writing about they tend to neglect developing them on paper. This happens because they naturally assume the reader knows what they know.

3. Over-explanation also becomes a problem. You tend to try and explain things too much, not allowing your reader to come to their own conclusion.

4. You limit your horizon because you already know how the story begins and ends.

5. Another one of the main problems that arise when writing a story based on real life events is that the writer fails to add detail that creates emotion. This happens because they are writing from their own experience instead of from the character's experience.

Don't get me wrong, the best urban novel writers often borrow from real life events. I do it in almost all of my books. The trick is to mix real life characters and stories with just the right amount of fiction. I've found that the best way to do this is by starting a scene with the real-life situation then letting it find its own way into fiction.

You must never allow your mind to be closed off to different possibilities. Maybe you really do have a good true story, most of us do. If this is the case then try writing it from a different character's point of view. Explore the use of third person narrative and watch yourself turn into another person.

Never allow yourself to be tied down by real life; leave your options open. Remember: in fiction, reality is only a small piece.

TURNING FACTS INTO FEELINGS

I can't emphasize enough that one of the most important rules about writing urban novels is to show instead of tell. If your goal is to write a realistic, believable story you need to show your character's feelings and thoughts. Give your reader a sense of how your character sees the world. In order for you to accomplish this goal you must first realize that, with creative writing, most of your formal teaching is wrong.

In school we learn to tell the teacher the facts we have learned from our lesson; to give answers from a purely logical point of view, keeping our feelings out of it. This is also how real life works in or day to day business dealings. But that's not the case when writing an urban novel.

When you embark on the journey of writing an urban novel the rules are completely different. You're not expected to state the facts like you do in a court of law. You gotta be aware of all your character's emotions and viewpoints regarding each individual situation he's presented with. Then you have to find the right words to paint the picture with so that your reader can become part of the whole experience. Think of it like this: instead of telling your readers how to feel, lead them in a way that will allow them to come to their own conclusions.

In life we sometimes have family or friends that try to protect us by giving us advice regarding real life experiences that we might be going through. Most of the time the advice is really good, but how many times do we actually listen? Sometimes you just have to learn life's lessons on your own. Well, urban novels are like that. You can definitely get your point across but you have to let the reader get to it on their own. The best way to accomplish this goal is by involving them in your story and letting them experience the world you have created for them. If you, do it right, nine times outta ten, they'll most likely come to the conclusion you intended them to from the beginning.

YOUR STORY HAS TO BE REALISTIC

In order to make your urban novel as realistic as possible you must create scenes that people can relate to. This can easily be done by appealing to all of their senses through words. You can do this by showing them instead of telling them. Here are four tips on how to show your reader what you want them to see, hear and feel:

1. Select a single character's point of view.
2. Know the thought process of that character at all times.
3. Present those thoughts and feelings as vividly as possible.
4. Give the reader these emotions at the right moment in time.

As long as you stay in the viewpoint of your main character, you will easily be able to show instead of tell. If you don't stay in viewpoint, you won't be able to "tell" the story because when real people experience life they don't "tell" about it, it just happens. This also helps to keep a certain level of thrill in your story because it gives the reader the sense that anything can happen at any time. And that's want you want; your ultimate goal is to have your reader experience the story as the characters do.

CHAPTER ONE

Blueprint

A blueprint is a detailed plan. The first mistake most novice writers make is they start their book without first creating a blueprint. Even I made this mistake during the outset of a few of my projects and it always creates undue problems that could've been thwarted if I would've just taken the time to write out a plan. With experience I've created a full-proof plan and I've split it into three sections, and they go in depth so pay attention to what you read in the next several pages because I'm really giving you some deep insight into the writing game.

PART 1: BACK TO BASICS

TITLE

You're gonna need a working title. A "working title" is the name you'll use to refer to your manuscript while you are writing it. This doesn't have to be the actual name that you go to the printing press with but it'll give you something to call it while you're working on it.

P.O.V.

The next step is figuring out what point of view you're gonna tell your story from. The best p.o.v. is a character who is closest to the action. The most important thing about p.o.v. is that you have to stay in it the whole time you write your story.

BLURB

Your blurb is a short sentence that summarizes the entire story. It should include the conflicts, goals and motivations of the star of your story. I'll cover this more in depth in the next chapter. After you write your blurb, post it up on the wall in front of your working area.

Just fill in the blanks: (name of protagonist) wants (goal to be achieved) because (motivation for acting), but he faces (conflict standing in the way).

STORY SPARKS

Now we need to come up with the beginning spark of your urban novel. "A spark" is a major conflict. Most urban novels start with a major conflict and go from there.

This first spark has to be a work of genius. This is what's gonna start the drama that will keep your urban novel going into the end. There will be other sparks but this first one has to be federal!

The average length of an urban novel is around 85,000 words. In a story of this length there should be at least three sparks. The first spark sets up the conflict. The middle spark complicates the situation and the last spark resolves the conflict and situation.

PART 2: WORKING DETAILS

The only way to have a cohesive story is to figure out all the working details, so let's cover 'em.

MAIN CHARACTERS

If you haven't came up with your main characters yet, this is the moment you get that done. Since you've gotten this far in preparing your urban novel, then you probably already know who the main players are going to be. This is when you should make a file for the characters that will include a checklist of information about them. Your characters will grow throughout the process of your writing, but these files will include a checklist of information on them including the basic information you'll need to start your book.

First, you need to introduce your character and that is basically listing your character's name and role in the story. Each of your main characters should bring something to the plot and this first introduction should explain that.

PHYSICAL DESCRIPTION

This description not only describes how your character looks but it also includes the impression he or she gives people when they first meet him. Does he look shady, trustworthy, scary or timid? There will be times in your urban novel when someone else is going to meet your protagonist and this description is what they'll see.

OCCUPATION DESCRIPTION

A lot of times, someone's job or hobby shapes their personality. Sometimes the plot of the story will revolve around their occupation; especially if it's drug dealing, gangbangin, prostitution or law enforcement.

ENHANCEMENTS AND CONTRAST

If you want to create a character who your readers will always remember, he's gonna need enhancements and contrasts. An enhancement is a character trait that makes your guy above average. You really don't want a protagonist who is average or your story will be boring. This doesn't have to be something obvious like the ability to fly, but is should set him apart from other people, and it doesn't have to come out early, either. He can utilize this skill when his back is against a wall.

The contrast is a personality flaw. It's never good to have characters who are 100% good or 100% bad. If you create a bad guy with some compassion, it will add depth to his personality. It's the same science with the good guy; he definitely shouldn't be all the way good because in real life no one is perfect.

People who read urban novels prefer a flawed star. It makes him realistic and they can relate to that. A strong contrast can be a secondary contrast which comes in the form of another character. If your protagonist is a level-headed individual who enters the drug world to make a certain amount of money, then gets out the game; a good contrast would be if he had a best friend who is a cold-blooded killer who lives for the fast life.

SYMBOLIC ELEMENT

A symbolic element is something that can be added to your story repeatedly that defines your main character or his arch-enemy in a subtle way. Every time it's mentioned it gains more meaning. This can be an object, event or emotion. It can also be a scar, a piece of jewelry or another character.

This symbol can be anything, but I'll give an example: Your character can be a vigilante who is adamant about ridding his neighborhood of drug dealers. His symbolic element can be a picture in his living room of his late mother who died of an overdose. Whenever he gets frustrated, all he has to do is look at the picture of his mother and he gets reinvigorated to do what he has set out to do.

The important thing that you need to keep in mind when

working with and/or creating a symbolic element is that it has to be subtle. You don't want to force it on your readers. And it's never too late to come up with this aspect of your story. You can always add it during the revision process.

SETTING

The setting of your story is important because it enhances the characters, the conflict and the suspense. It also provides a landscape for your story to unfold. If the setting for your story doesn't match the plot you'll have a harder time trying to create the right mood for your urban novel.

In order to paint a vivid picture to your readers you need to describe a setting to your story. It has to match though. Can you imagine an urban novel taking place on a space ship? It wouldn't match because it's not the right genre for that setting.

You want to set your story in a place that you can persuade your readers to believe really exists. Even if it's a fictional location it should be realistic and match your storyline. Another thing you should keep in mind is that you only need to describe the parts that involve the plot of your urban novel. There's no point in describing things that don't move the story along.

PART 3: DRAMA

If you want a realistic, interesting plot, you're gonna need some conflict. Without conflict there's no story. I'm gonna go ahead and lace you on the aspect of conflicts so pay attention. You'll need the following items for all of your sparks, and you should also include these situations for all of your major characters.

INTERNAL CONFLICT

In urban novels, character conflicts are what keep the characters from accomplishing their goals. He can't solve his problem until he faces his conflicts. Your audience must also be able to identify with these conflicts in order for them to be involved with the story.

Internal conflicts are emotional problems that conflict with the character's conscious. This is what keeps your character stubborn and from seeing the obvious.

If you don't recognize this conflict early your story won't be as organized as it should be. The drama will bounce around and confuse your reader because your urban novel will be flooded with unfocused ideas. Conflicts that aren't identified clearly will bore your reader and that's what you don't want.

Your first spark is the one that'll show your reader what your character's conflicts are. It's usually connected to something or someone your character cares about passionately. It could be something or someone who your character loves who is in danger of being hurt or lost. This will motivate your character to keep pushing until he saves what he loves.

Internal conflicts are different from external ones. But at the same time, you can't have one without the other. A story with external conflicts but no internal ones is like an old-school black and white cartoon next to the pixel animation of today. Your internal conflicts are all about the characters and the external conflicts revolve around the plot. What they should have in common is that they should both belong to the main character. If they don't, they shouldn't be part of his or her story.

EVOLVING GOALS AND MOTIVATIONS

Goals are what the protagonist (the main character) wants, needs or desires more than anything else in the world. Motivation is what gives him the drive to complete his goals. Your main character has to want to accomplish his goal so bad that he's willing to kill, steal and destroy for it.

Different goals from multiple characters are meant to collide because it creates conflict and conflict is always good. If you have a protagonist (main character) and an antagonist (main character's enemy) whose goals bump heads, as long as they both feel passionately about their own agendas– you got the makings of one helluva plot.

One of the ways to make your story super interesting is to make your main character somehow have to go against his morals to accomplish this goal. This will force him to grow, and at the same time give him an opportunity to change. This needs to happen every time there is a story spark. The best urban novels grow organically from cause and effect. This means that, every time your character goes through something, he's put into a situation where he has to make a decision that may force him to grow into a deeper person; as well as placing him in another conflict.

PLOT CONFLICTS

Plot conflicts are the big problems that stand in the way of your protagonist accomplishing his goals. He or she has to overcome said obstacle or else the story will not move forward. Plot conflicts need immediate action. Like your guy getting something back that was taken from him or resolving the issue that he was faced with. Internal conflicts are what hurts him on the inside, like the vigilante whose mother died of an overdose.

It might go against his morals to kill people; but because his adversary, the neighborhood kingpin is sending people to kill him, he has to react in order to save himself.

The plot conflicts are the hired hitters who the kingpin has sent to kill him. The information that I've been giving you throughout these last few pages are building blocks for your urban novel. It's up to you to put them together in a way that will bring your story to life.

CHAPTER TWO

Let's Get it Crackin'

Do you got the three D's??? Determination; Discipline; and Dedication?

The fact is that anyone with the right training can write an urban novel. The problem is that most people aren't willing to take the time out of their lives to sit down and do it. There is actually only a small percentage of people who make their dreams come to fruition. If you want to be one of the individuals who make your dreams come true, you'll have to have the three D's.

You'll need determination to overcome the unforeseen obstacles that will definitely materialize once you get started. You'll also need discipline to work on your project every day. And dedication is necessary if you plan on seeing your project all the way to the end.

If you have what it takes then what I'm about to give you will enable you to get started within ten days. If you follow the plan that I'm about to layout for you, you'll be in the best situation possible before you even start on this mission. Later on, we'll cover aspects of writing, such as craft and skill, but right now we gotta get you started the right way.

Your first step in this ten-day process is setting up your very own corner. This will be the spot where nothing else will happen except your writing. It needs to be nice, quiet and comfortable. A place where you can safely leave your notes, laptop or computer.

The next step is setting up a schedule. You'll have to commit at least one hour out of your day to making this happen. It has to be a time of your day with the least amount of distractions. Did I mention the fact that you'll be doing this all week?

DAY 1. Today is the day you announce what your story will be about. Every story starts out from a seed; you need to ask yourself what your urban novel is going to be about. After you do that, jot down all of your ideas. You'll need characters and some sort of struggle or plot. Your goal is to isolate your story and define it in one sentence. After you accomplish this, write your sentence on a piece of paper and tape it on the wall above your desk. This way it'll always be visible when you work.

DAY 2. Now that we've made it to your second day it's time for a casting call. Every urban novel has a cast of characters and today is when you begin your roll call. You'll need to make a list of characters and put them under headings such as major and minor roles. Then describe how they know one another. Don't worry about physical or emotional description. That will come later. Put these notes to the side and you're done for today.

DAY 3. Today we work on locations. You'll need to make a list of cities, towns, houses or apartments where major scenes will take place. It doesn't matter if the spots are made up or not, just list your locations. Don't worry about the descriptions, that'll come later on as well. Once you finish with this you'll be done for the day.

DAY 4. Today we go back to your list of characters. Every main character should want something he can't have. They should all have specific goals that motivates them and gives them the three D's. Regardless of how high their goals are or whether they can accomplish them or not, they should still want them. As soon as you figure them out, summarize them in one sentence. Each character should have three goals. When you finish with this, put it away. You're done for the day.

DAY 5. So far, we've listed the main characters and their goals. Today we are going to list the obstacles that will get in the way of your characters accomplishing their goals. The obstacles can be anything from other characters to emotional or physical issues. Just like they had three goals, they'll need three obstacles. This is how an urban novel gains structure. You can put everything away for the day once you've finished.

DAY 6. Now it's time to create an ending to your story. Come up with a good conclusion and either write it out in paragraph form, or point form. Once you've done that, tape it on the wall right next to the sentence you posted up on your first day of working this project. However, keep in mind that sometimes characters have a mind of their own. While you're writing, things might change and you'll end up with an ending that you didn't plan on in the beginning. So don't feel locked in to this ending. You're doing this to keep yourself grounded.

DAY 7. Today you'll be making an outline for your story. Make a list of all the major scenes in your book but don't worry about the details. This is an important phase in the preparation of your urban novel. On the days when you feel like you have writer's block you can go back to this list and pick and choose what you want to write about. Since you'll have this list you will be able to write about anything that you choose. You can always fill in the transition scenes later, that's nothing.

It's starting to get real now, huh?

DAY 8. Today we go back to the outline you did yesterday and separate your major scenes into chapters. You're gonna make a list of chapter titles and no more than two sentences describing the major events that take place in each chapter. After you make this list I want you to tape it on the wall next to the other things you already put up there.

You gotta trust me on this. The moves you're making now are essential to the writing process. It's like creating an elaborate map to the promise land.

DAY 9. Today you'll be setting up your files. This is how all your information is going to get organized. It'll make everything easy to locate whenever your mind goes blank. Whenever you open up one of these files you'll automatically have something to write about. Each folder will need to be labeled so you will know what it contains.

Here's the list of files:

CHARACTERS: You'll need full, detailed descriptions of their physical characteristics, emotional needs and family background. Later on, I'll lace you with more game on how to build characters. In the end, you'll end up with more than enough information to fill these files.

LOCATIONS: It's extremely important to your readers that you place them inside the world of your urban novel. Your goal should be to take them off of their couch and into the world of your characters. The only way you'll be able to accomplish this is by painting pictures with words. Paint these pictures then place your art into this folder

INDIVIDUAL CHAPTERS: In this file you'll be storing all the notes on each individual chapter. Let's say you just wrote a scene out of order and you have an idea on how you want it transitioned, this is where you'll store information like that.

MANNERISMS: If you sit back and watch people, you'll start to notice the different things they do to express their emotions. Anyone can write about how happy a character was when he copped his first kilo of cocaine; but wouldn't it be more intense if you described how the character held his breath in anticipation while the kilo's wrapping was being taken off? And how he and his crew started jumping around, high-fiving one another once they saw that it was A-1 fish scale? That's what I did when I got my first brick. It makes it real! This is where you'll store those ideas so you can add them in later.

SPEACH PATTERNS: Dialogue is a very important part of storytelling. Knowing speech patterns is a significant aspect of writing. Think of how someone like Lil Wayne talks versus Paris Hilton. They both talk differently even though they are both speaking the same language. If your story takes place in New York, but your main character is from Tennessee, his speech will naturally be different than the Puerto Rican guy at the local bodega. It helps by giving each of your characters different speech patterns; like favorite phrases or different ways of expressing themselves.

GENERAL OBSERVATIONS: Sometimes you might have a thought about your story that doesn't fit with what you're working on at the time. It's important that you write those thoughts down and file them in this folder. You never know when you might be able to use it, so put it here for now.

DAY 10. Man, we finally reached day 10. You've set up your work area, wrote out an outline and organized your project. Today is the day you'll break ground on your urban novel by writing out the opening paragraph. This paragraph has to be intriguing so the reader will crave for more–like a drug. It's best to start the story right when your main character is faced with a major dilemma. There are three main points that should always be included in your opening paragraph.

1.   The main character.
2.   His/her situation.
3.   Some details to show your readers how deep in the shit the character is really in.

You should always have something to write about after you finish these first ten days. All you have to do is go through your folders and find something to write about, even if it's just describing characters, locations, mannerisms, speech patterns or other things in your files. Remember, you don't have to write your urban novel in order.

Now you have a guide so you can write whatever you want, whenever you want.

It's up to you to set your own goals, if you write two pages a day, you'll have your book done in six months. If you work longer hours, you'll finish a lot sooner. It's all on you. Now that you are finally ready to get started, let's get it crackin'!

CHAPTER THREE

Gems for your bag of tricks

The only way to become a great urban novel author is by writing. It's just like that jump shot; you have to keep practicing if you wanna be the best. How many hours have you sat in front of that X Box trying to beat your favorite game? Those skills didn't come from the instruction manual, they came from practice. A lot of improvement will come one sentence at a time, one paragraph at a time, one page and so on. It might seem tedious, but in the end, you'll see that you've become a professional writer with the skills that set you apart from the masses.

And it's only gonna happen if you make it happen. Writing an urban novel isn't a goal that you can go after half-steppin'. You must set aside a time of day, every day, so you can sit down and write. People in your life need to know about your goal and they need to understand that during this designated time your world is not to be interrupted. If you're serious about this then you're gonna have to discipline yourself. This type of work ethic is what'll set you apart from all those people who think they can sit down and write an urban novel any time they feel like it.

I'm gonna give you a gem right now, so pay attention and get ready to file it away for later use. There are two different writing times; I call them "plotting" and "scheming."

Plotting is when you're actually in front of your laptop or

typewriter writing the words down. This is when your work is really being done. Then there's the time I call scheming, and this is anytime you're just thinking about what you're gonna write. You can do this anywhere, anytime of the day or night. From while you're taking a shit, to the driver's seat of your car, on your way to work ... you can scheme anywhere.

I believe scheming is a tool that all writers should use in their writing process. Whenever things seem to get hard and your brain locks up, just back up for a minute; take a stroll up the block and let your thoughts provoke you. The mind is a wonderful thing and sometimes you gotta let it do what it does. Instead of sitting at your desk beating yourself up because you can't seem to come up with any ideas, pull back and go from plotting to scheming.

OH, NOW YOU CAN'T FIND THE TIME, HUH???

Yeah, it's a trip how at times we can become our own worst enemy. You have the idea for a great urban novel, you have determination, discipline and dedication, but all of sudden when you see how much work it's gonna take, you just can't seem to find the time to do it. Ain't that something...

In case you come into a problem like this, here's a few ideas on how you can navigate through your daily routine:

1. Stay up an hour later. At night, there's less disturbances because everyone else is either tired or asleep. It's not gonna effect you if you stay up one hour later every night. You'll most likely get extra energy when you're doing something you are passionate about.

2. Start your day an hour earlier. If you get up an hour earlier than you usually do, everyone around you will still be asleep. Therefore, you'll have a nice, quiet time to get your work done.

3.   If you have a job, use the time on the way to work to get your writing done. A lot of people take the bus or train to work. This is a great time to pullout the laptop. However, if you're driving you might want to get an app for your phone so you can record your ideas. Regardless, the time you take to get to work is usually a time when you're away from the rest of the world: utilize it!

4.   Since we're talking about work, why not use your lunch hour? Most people get paid during their lunch hour, why not pack a bag lunch and get paid to write your urban novel?

5.   Take a look at your evenings. I know people who dedicate their Friday and Saturday nights to club hopping. Is there a night of the week when you can go somewhere and do nothing but work on your urban novel? You'll be surprised at how much work you can get accomplished in just 3 hours a week.

6.   What about your weekends? How many Saturday afternoons have you spent just lounging around the house? That time can easily be put aside for writing your urban novel.

7.   Take a look at your off time. Is there a time of your day when you spend watching reruns? The TV is a dummy box. Sometimes you spend so many hours a day watching nothing, and that time can easily be used to creating your masterpiece!

If you're really serious about creating a great story, stop coming up with excuses and let's do this! The time is there, all you need is effort.

CHAPTER FOUR

Make it unique

The only way to set your urban novel apart from the others is by showing your passion. Make your reader *feel* what they are reading. Whatever makes you happy, sad or angry can make your characters happy, sad and angry. The same things that inspire you can also inspire your characters.

I've put together an exclusive questionnaire that will enable you to pull the most passion out of your characters. This is an assignment that you can file away and use throughout your writing process. I have several questions that you'll need to answer. Before you start, you'll need to clear your mind. The only thought on your mental should revolve around your story. As soon as you read these questions, I want you to write down the first thing that comes to mind:

1.   Are your characters real? Is your story believable?
2.   Does your character have feelings? Does anyone in your story have a cause?
3.   Who is the hero? Who needs to be saved?
4.   When you think of your story, what makes you mad? What's happening behind the scenes? Is there an unseen question?
5.   Can you create a scene where the main character has

to defend something? Preferably when everyone thinks he's wrong? Why should we care about him/her?

A common setback in most urban novels is that the main character often becomes too far above average. Sometimes this makes the reader doubt the whole story because of the unrealistic situations the main character overcomes. This is why it's important that you humanize your characters; so that your readers will be able to relate to them and believe in them. Here's some more questions, and remember, this exercise isn't just for the fun of it; you should find places in your story where you can incorporate all of this information.

1. Find something in your main character's life that everyone has experienced and can relate to. Then add it in early in the story.

2. Is there something in your urban novel that people of all walks of life can relate to? If not, it'll help if you can add something that's universal.

3. What does your main character do that everyone else does too? Does he have any superstitions? Is there something he learned from his mother or father?

4. There has to be a situation that becomes overwhelming for your main character. And make him admit it.

A lot of urban novel authors like to make their novels portray a message of sorts. That's cool, yet making your story an outlet to preach your message can sometimes become a problem. No one wants to escape their daily lives by reading a sermon. The best way to get your point across is through the plot. Allow your plot to become the teacher and let the character be the student.

Here's how you can slip your message in nonchalantly:

1. What is the message you're trying to convey?
2. At what point in the story does your main character realize something is wrong?
3. Is there anyone in your story that can change their outlook on life by the end of the book?
4. Is your main character better off by the end of the story?
5. Is there anyone in your urban novel that doesn't see the solution to the main problem of the story?

If you can incorporate all these ideas into your story your urban novel will be more intense. It will add depth to your writing. Little details like these are what will enable the reader to become more involved in the whole intake process. Ergo, making the experience more satisfying.

CHAPTER FIVE

You reap what you sow

Think of an idea like a weed seed. You get a seed and plant it, and after you plant it you must nurture it so you can get that thick, healthy bud. Ideas for urban novels are the same way. Ideas can come in the form of a character, theme, an overheard dialogue or a newsreel. Ideas are everywhere and your job is to search the world for the best seeds.

The best place to look for ideas is in your own life. If you can't see 'em, you might have to look a little harder. You can turn anything you experience into a great story. Home life, personal relationships, people in your neighborhood, or things that happen at work can make great story fodder. All you have to do is open your mind and look around. Sometimes all you have to do is search your own mind. What is it that you really like and what is it that you really love? These two opposites can ignite a great story. And remember: just because you started a story with a real story doesn't mean you have to stick to the truth. That situation was only a seed for your plant. Now you have to nurture it so it'll grow into a whole urban novel.

One of the reasons that drive people to read urban novels is their chance to enter other people's lives. We may never meet El Chapo, but your urban novel might let your reader spend a day in his life. It's almost as if we're listening in on someone's phone conversation. You shouldn't be doing it, but do you really want to hang up the phone?

The best part is when your reader finds out that the infamous El Chapo is a normal person. He falls in love, he gets sad, has hobbies and even has a few secrets just like them. The best writers are those who can show these human attributes in people who are usually untouchable. The way you do this is by recognizing the seeds that are floating around in your life.

Once you learn how to recognize these seeds, you're now looking at the world through the eyes of a writer. After you realize this you'll go from not having ideas to write about to having so many stories that you couldn't possibly write about all of them.

It's up to you to pick and choose the right seed. And only you can decide which one is the "one." The best thing to do if you think you just found the perfect seed is to write it down. Every writer should have a notebook set aside just for ideas because even though you might not see it right now, it'll be put up for that moment when you can turn it into something.

One idea isn't gonna write a whole urban novel, either. Don't forget that. It takes imagination to write a whole book. You're gonna have to nurture that idea just like you would a weed plant. The main goal in writing urban novels is to have someone else enjoy your story. The stranger doesn't care where you found the seed or how much time you put into growing it, he just wants to smoke the final product!

At one time or another, everybody feels like they have a story to tell. After reading the last few pages, you should have come to the understanding that ideas come like a passing wind. The truth of the matter is that not many people get their ideas on paper and even fewer people write their stories and go through the several drafts that it takes to fine-tune that novel. For an urban novel to exist it has to be written. For it to be any good, the author has to put in a lot of work. This is the part of the writing process that the average person never sees. You just need to be dedicated and the rest will fall into place.

So, allow me to digress for a moment just to make sure you have what I'm trying to convey:

1. In order for you to create an intriguing urban novel you're gonna have to create characters that your readers will care about as well as relate to. If you can come up with everyday situations that your characters will be in and experience their emotions, then that's true imagination.

2. A true author must understand what makes their readers tick. You have to have some insight into the human mind so that you'll know why people do the things they do. You're gonna need compassion and be willing to understand and express different points of view.

3. Once you create a character, you're gonna need to understand him better than anyone else and have the skills to express this in print. You're gonna have to put his feelings and thought process on paper so that your readers will understand why he does the things he does. Always remember: No one is always good or always bad.

4. The only way you're gonna create a character that your readers will truly care about is by making the reader believe the character really exists.

5. Every well-written urban novel has a mixture of plot, structure and action. If you want to write a good book it's gonna have to be a page turner so you'll have to zero in on these three aspects.

6. A plot is a storyline. If you want to test yourself to see if you're any good at creating plots, pick any event in your life and try to unravel it into a whole story plot in ten pages or less. If you can do this in less than an hour, then you're a natural.

7. When writing a story you're gonna need to paint a picture and inject a mood as well as a sense of time. The best

urban novels can take their readers from their reality into the inside of the book.

8.   Dialogue is important for any story because it helps move the plot along. It also shows the character of a person and separates one character from another. The best dialogue does this and sounds realistic all at the same time. If your dialogue doesn't do this, then get rid of it because it can ruin your whole urban novel.

9.   If you want your book to have an authentic feeling you might have to do some homework on your subjects. If you're not from the place your plot is set, then you're gonna have to learn the streets because one mistake can throw your reader off and make him close your book.

These are all tricks of the trade. A person with no formal training in writing wouldn't be expected to know all these things, and even though said person might have mad creative skills when writing, without these gems they'll never shine at their fullest potential.

CHAPTER SIX

Control Your Ideas

If you're anything like I am you probably have a treasure trove full of ideas about stories. That's good, and that's why you should have a notebook handy where you can jot down your thoughts. The only time having so many different ideas becomes a problem is when you try to stuff them all under one platform. If you plan on writing a superior urban novel you will have to remain grounded. If you don't control your ideas you will run the risk of losing your reader and that's the worst thing that you can ever do.

Nothing is better than coming up with a new idea for a book. Nevertheless, before you get it on paper you're going to need to come up with a game plan. The main objective is to get your readers to open your book and enjoy what they read. You don't want to have things slowing down the pace. Here are four ideas to keep in mind while writing your urban novel:

1. Start your story with the main character. Within the first 300 words the reader should meet the main character and have a reason to care about him or her.
2. Transport the reader into your world. Immediately let the reader know where he's at and when he's there. The setting is extremely important. The reader will get confused

if he doesn't know where he's at or what era the story is taking place in. Whenever the consumer gets confused or bored the first thing he does is put the book the down, sometimes forever.

3. Explain your point. After you introduce the main player you must let your readers know where he's at. Next, you let them know why they should care. There has to be some sort of mission at hand. Let your reader know what the character wants and what he's willing to do to get it.

4. Stay focused. If you ever start to go off on a tangent, stop. Go back to your original idea. Yes, readers do have a mind of their own. However, no one wants to go halfway through a story just to find out that everything they've read up to that point had nothing to do with where they're at now.

The best way to go about controlling your ideas is by controlling your environment. It's really hard to stay focused when you have music playing, phones ringing and a TV blaring. If you're planning on writing an urban novel you're gonna have to take your project seriously. Let those around you know how much your goals mean to you, this way they will respect your working time more. When you set up a certain time of the day to write, it means you will be cutting yourself off from the rest of the world. An ideal area is a room where you can shut the door. It needs to be a sanctuary where you can go and not have to worry about distractions.

Don't panic when things don't seem to be going your way. Just write! No matter what, keep writing! Don't worry about your spelling, grammar or editing when you're writing your first draft. You'll have plenty of time to edit later. Prepare yourself for the days you have writer's block. It comes with the terrain. Some days you'll do the damn thang and write crazy pages, but then there will be those days when your mental goes blank. When this happens, don't trip. That's what the files are there for. You can always take a break, too. There's never a problem with taking a sabbatical, as long as it doesn't come right when you have a deadline coming.

While you're writing, don't get caught up in trying to share your work with other people. As soon as you ask someone what they think about your work, the first thing they'll do is try to write their own story through you. Before you go around asking for advice, finish your first draft.

And don't try to steal the next man's swagger. What some people do is find an author they like and try to imitate that author's style of writing. If you ever want to reach your peak you're gonna have to find your own mojo. Anyone can detect a fake and no one respects a knock-off. People appreciate originality.

Also, keep in mind that when you are writing an urban novel you are creating art. After it's finished, it then becomes a product. You need to remember to separate the two distinctions.

While you are writing you need all your concentration centered on being the best writer you can be. You mustn't allow your mind to drift because you're worried about sales.

Just strive to do your best. In the end, people will enjoy it ... you'll see.

CHAPTER SEVEN

Craft

Now it's time to start discussing the different aspects of craft. In case you don't understand the meaning of the word "craft," it's like learning a trade; it's a unique set of skills that will help you get your story on paper properly.

Well-written urban novels come down to craft a lot more than people realize. This is why so many people take the writing process for granted. Yeah, anybody can write a story; just like anyone can paint a house. But there is a major difference between writers with skill and knowledge on the writing craft, and those who have never had any form of formal training. Let's use the painter analogy: there's a big difference between someone who paints houses and someone who paints portraits. It takes a lot more artistry to accomplish the latter.

If you want to be known for good urban novels then you'll have to learn these skills. It's the only way you'll be able to accumulate a following. For the record: I wasn't the man who invented the rules on this craft, but I can lace you with an outline so you can learn it. That's what this book is all about, learning the craft of writing and getting rich and famous off the skills you obtain.

Here's a quick peek into what I'm talking about: Let's say you're writing a story about a certified Ho-Bitch. If you're following the rules of craft you will understand that it's better to "show" instead of "tell." Therefore, you know that you will need to create a scene to show she's a ho. Having her turn a trick, bring back the money to her pimp, then go back out to pull another trick is a great way to "show" that she's a prostitute, isn't it? As a matter of fact, this is what I'm talking about right here. This is a scene straight out of my first urban book, *Devils & Demons...*

Five o'clock took forever to come. Alize spent the day stalking the clock. She thought she had it all planned out. So that she wouldn't seem thirsty she told herself that she wouldn't answer the phone the first time Talton called. Her plan didn't work, though.

The moment she got in her car, her phone vibrated and she answered it immediately. It was Talton, so she told him to meet her at the McDonalds up the street from Show Girls. She told him she'd be there at six, giving herself an hour to get ready.

When she got home, she barely got through the front door before she started stripping down. Dropping clothes everywhere, she was completely naked by the time she reached the bathroom. Then, as she went to turn on the water, she caught a glimpse of herself in the mirror that hung from the door. Her bushy, red pubic hair stared back at her defiantly. In the last several months she had neglected to shave her private areas because she didn't have anyone to impress. Things had changed, though; it was time to clean up the yard.

When the water hit the right temperature, she stepped in, letting the warm stream run down her body. After a few moments she reached for a bar of soap and started soaping up her pubic region, getting it ready for the razor. As she was doing this, she accidently rubbed her fingers across her clitoris. This triggered an avalanche of erotic stimuli. Her whole day had been spent thinking about a man whom she was extremely attracted to. Unable to ease the sexual tension, she settled for a private message triggered by rocking her thighs back and forth.

But, right now, in the shower, with her finger between her thighs, she could no longer help herself. After that initial brush with her love button, the rest was a wrap. She quickly began masturbating, fast and hard. Since she was in a rush, she treated herself roughly. Feverishly attacking her silky folds with her soapy fingers. At one point, she almost lost her footing, so she placed her free hand on the wall to steady herself as she violently penetrated her nether regions.

Alize's heart was beating wildly, her breath became short and her knees started to shake. An orgasm was mounting; this made Ze switch gears. With the tip of three fingers, she stroked her swollen clitoris as fast as humanly possible. Then she felt it coming. With her eyes closed, she visualized the man of her dreams. At the moment the waves of ecstasy overcame her body, she made a conscious decision to make Talton the father of her next child...

Creating a scene that shows your character's traits allows your readers to come to their own conclusions about who they are reading about. At the same time, it takes them deeper into the story than if you would've just told them she was a ho. This alone will add authenticity to your urban novel. Once you start thinking like this on your own, then you'll begin to master the craft of writing urban novels.

At the same time, I want to note something else: even though the rules of craft are tried and true and they have been tested time and time again doesn't mean that you can't go outside the box. The world is full of people who have dared to think outside of the box. If you're a beast you might come up with a new way to accomplishing the same goal. Personally, I'd take the route that made the best writers into millionaires, but if you got a gut feeling about something, I recommend that you do you.

It might take you a few times of reading this book in order to get all the rules down. The least you'll need to do is keep this book around while you write so you can always go back to it for reference. The important thing is to understand that in order for you to write a good urban novel, you'll have to learn the lessons in this book.

While I'm at it, I want to remind you to read, read and read some more. Anytime you see an urban novel, pick it up and read it! You never know where you might find a new idea or skill. If you're reading a book and you find yourself getting bored or confused, ask yourself why. Is the plot unrealistic? Do you care about the characters? Sometimes you can learn more from a book you don't like than one you do.

The moment you begin to understand the rules of craft you'll begin to realize that your stories will reach a new level of enjoyment. You'll enter the ranks of all the great writers. Creating stories that tickle, torment, intrigue and entertain your readers. When it's all said and done, you did that! You accomplished all that with words on paper and that's something to be proud of.

CHAPTER EIGHT

Plot

The plot of your story is what your characters do to overcome their obstacles. All of this has to be in progression towards the final resolution. It must follow cause and effect guidelines which we'll get into deeper in the following pages. Just know that the plot is the meat of your story.

Most plots are based on a problem that the average person will never experience. That's what makes it so interesting. It gives your reader a way to escape their own world to enter yours. Based on the fact that the obstacles are so extraordinary the job of the author becomes something like playing chess with an alter ego. You'll have to figure out what resourceful, surprising, yet believable things your main character will have to do next in order to overcome his or her problem. This is definitely the part that the readers love the most. A well written urban novel can be transformational. You want the reader to see and sense the transformation of the main characters as they read the story. The plot isn't just about one thing leading into another, it's about watching the main character grow and learn.

A major blunder that most novice writers make is creating stories with BOSH type plots. "BOSH" stands for "Bunch of Shit Happens." No one likes reading a story where a gang of bullshit takes place without any type of structure to it.

Everything that takes place in your story should lead into the next scene. These are the plots that are referred to as tightly woven; it's the best way to write a story because the tension grows as the story gains momentum. If you can write a story with these attributes, the end result will be a page turner.

A common problem all writers experience is plotting. It happens to seasoned craftsmen as well as beginners. The problems start when the main character doesn't want to do what he has to for him to overcome his obstacles. The reason this happens is because the writer (You) tends to grow too close to the character and tries to solve all the problems himself. This happens when you become too involved in your story, like it's actually you who is in the world that you've created. You can't do that. Remember, it's your character who is facing the problem – not you.

Great plots reach their peaks because of the opposing characters. Nevertheless, this only happens when those characters are created well. Your reader must know the characters so good that they begin to empathize with them. Once you create some memorable players and pit them against one another, your story is really going to start getting interesting.

This is when the reader will hate putting the book down. As soon as you establish some deep characters, your plot will automatically unfold itself. Then all you have to do is create a situation where they'll go at each other and your plot will come alive.

A perfect example of what I'm talking about is the TCB book, *To Live & Die in L.A.* by Mike Enemigo and Anthony Murillo. Anthony goes through just the right amount of time introducing his main character, Fast Eddie, so that you know he's a car thief who gets money and fucks bitches, but not much else. So, when he and his homeboy, Bullet, car jacks some dude for his SUV and they find over a million dollars' worth of heroin in the truck, the reader believes it when the problems start arising.

Well, Eddie isn't a drug dealer, neither is his friend, so they have to go outside of their circle to try and get rid of it and that's when they find themselves in an unlikely alliance with a member of the Mexican Mafia. On top of that, the drugs actually belonged to a Mexican drug lord who has a biker gang working for him. That means not only does Eddie have problems getting rid of the illicit contraband, he also has an army of professional criminals after him. It's all cause and effect.

I want you to give me a moment and sit back and think of your favorite urban novel. I'm talking about one you tried to read in one sitting. That particular story most likely had crazy plot structure. One event led to another which ended up creating another situation that was more interesting than the last one. That's how you get someone involved in your story. Have 'em sitting at the edge of their seat, rushing to turn the page to find out what happens next. The core of a book like that is the excitement one feels while reading it. That's what you should thrive for as a writer.

The only way you're gonna be able to accomplish this is through the plot. A strong plot is what brings everything together. All the characters, the settings and the voice of the story come together by way of plot.

Every plot has a question that needs to be answered. That question is going to need a straight up Yes or No answer. Will Fast Eddie get rid of the stolen drugs? Will the Mexican Mafia goon turn on him before it's all said and done? These are the types of questions that should be the bottom line of your story. And you must create a story that will make your reader care about the answer.

It does not matter what the main answer is as long as it's realistic. Along the process of writing your urban novel you will create a character that your reader will grow to know. The outcome of the story has to realistically match what the character you have created is actually capable of accomplishing. If you can convince your reader of this, you have done your job.

Readers don't want to finish a book with the feeling that the ending was fake. I remember reading an urban novel that had realistic characters and plot structure throughout the whole story, but then in the end they somehow got their hands on a military grade laser and used it to kill all the drug dealers on the East Coast. That shit was totally unrealistic and it ruined the story for me. It left such a bad taste in my mouth that I made a conscious decision to never ever read another book by that author. Readers want an ending that they can believe came from the characters they've met and grew to love or hate throughout the story. Not some unimaginable ending the author scraped together in fifteen minutes.

Don't forget that main question. If your whole urban novel is about Jeezy taking over his neighborhood, the reader isn't going to care if his paperboy saved up enough money to buy a video game. They want to know if blood takes over his 'hood. Ergo, you must, above all, remain focused.

The main character in any story is called the Protagonist. The protagonist will be the most important person in your story. In *To Live & Die in L.A.*, readers get to know Fast Eddie better than anyone else in the story. Therefore, the main question in that novel is centered around him. He is the protagonist.

Most plots are focused on the number one desire of the protagonist. The whole plot is driven by this goal. His desire can be conscious, where he knows what he wants. Or unconscious, where he doesn't really know what he wants. Either way, your reader will know and this is what they'll care about.

Now, remember, plots center around conflict. Conflicts are created by the obstacles that are set in your character's way. It's what keeps him from accomplishing his main goal in life.

Conflicts materialize in many forms. Some of them are

external, like the antagonist. The antagonist is the protagonists' arch-enemy or anyone who constantly tries to stop him from getting what he wants.

Other obstacles are internal, they happen inside your character's mind. In the case at hand, Eddie doesn't trust his ally, the Mexican Mafia goon, but in order for him to be able to sell the stolen drugs he has to stay close to him because he can't do it by himself. In this case, the struggle takes place mostly inside of his head. Stories that really involve the reader usually have an internal struggle.

Most urban novels have more than one or two of these conflicts. It makes a good story because it's what the readers want. Even though it is all hurtful towards the protagonist it makes a good story. Also, a well written complication will either illuminate, thwart or change what the main character wants. A strong conflict will put emotional pressure on the protagonist, forcing him to not only move mean, but to move with meaning. If the conflict doesn't create this atmosphere, it's not a conflict.

A strong problem can add weight to your story as well. For instance, let's say a drug dealer had to run from the police, and in the process he loses his sack. Now his problem is that he has to make up for the loss he just took. How many pages is it gonna take for you to state that problem and then fix it?

Let's say that same dope boy had to throw away that same sack of dope, but now you add in the fact that the drugs were actually fronted to him and he now owes someone. On top of that, he only has a certain amount of time to pay up; and the only way he can come up with type of revenue is by robbing other drug dealers. That will give the problem a lot more urgency, at the same time, adding more pages/content to your manuscript.

If you want, you can also break down a plot into three sections; just like a chess game. The beginning, the middle and the end. The beginning of every urban novel should do three things: You must drop your reader into a major scene.

Second, you have to provide your reader with all the necessary information to let them know what's going on and what led to that situation. The third thing you have to provide is the major question that the whole plot will be based on.

Don't start your story when everything is normal. That would be boring. The whole point of reading an urban novel is to be transported into a new and exciting world. But since you're going to start your story right in the middle of the action, you will have to give it a backstory. You will have to explain to your readers what is happening and why it's happening. Don't give 'em everything all at once, but give them enough so that they'll want more. Then hit them with the question. And after they're up on game about what's going on, that's when you'll let them know what the protagonist will be fighting for. Now, that's the beginning of a great urban novel!

The beginning of your story will most likely overlap with the middle and that's what's supposed to happen. The middle is where you really show your readers who your main character truly is; this is where you'll develop your protagonist. This is also where the meat of your story is located. The middle of your story is way longer than the beginning and the end because it involves all of the obstacles your antagonist will place in the way of your main character. The middle of your urban novel should almost seem like a graph, where the tensions of the conflicts rise until it can't realistically rise any further. You have to build the tension and conflict so high that it becomes an all-out crisis.

You must, at all cost, stay away from creating random obstacles. Those conflicts tend to be unrealistic and your readers will see right through it. The best conflicts come from a sort of cause and effect. When your main character was faced with his problem, he reacted a certain way, which created another conflict, and so on, until things got out of control. But the thing is, throughout your story, even though the conflicts are becoming harder, your main character should be growing and becoming wiser. This is something that really happens to us when our backs are against a wall in real life. This will keep the protagonist humanized.

The ending of an urban novel is actually the shortest part. This is the section where everything pieces together. The end of an urban novel usually follows a pattern that most writers refer to as their three C's. Crisis, Climax and Consequences. The crisis is when that tension hits its highest form. The climax is when that tension breaks and you finally receive the answer to that main question that the whole plot was based on. And the consequence is the final ending. No matter how short it may be, it's the point where all the loose ends are tied together.

A good ending should be realistic, yet unexpected. If your reader can tell how the book is gonna end, there is no point in having them read it. You have to surprise your reader. However, at the same time, your ending has to make sense. So, when they look back on the story they'll see that the whole story was heading in that direction since the beginning.

TEN GEMS

1. The plot is what your characters do to overcome their obstacles in a progression towards a resolution.

2. The plot isn't just about one thing leading to another, but also about the main character learning and growing.

3. Once you create some memorable characters and you "pit" them against each other is when your story will start to get interesting.

4. Every plot needs a question that needs a "yes" or "no" answer.

5. Your main character is called your protagonist and his arch-enemy is called the antagonist.

6. Obstacles can be internal as well as external.

7. Never start your story when everything is normal.

8. The best conflicts come from cause and effect.

9. 3 C's: Crisis, Climax and Consequence.
10. A good ending should be realistic but unexpected!

CHAPTER NINE

Characters

In the last chapter I wrote about plot. I'm hoping you took from that and filed it away because that subject is actually the cornerstone of the writing process. Now, we'll be covering the subject of characters and how to build them up so your readers will remember your stories years after they've read them. Building your characters is important because they are the center of your story. The characters in your urban novel are what makes people care about what's happening. They drive the story from beginning to end.

An experienced author can make his readers believe the characters in their stories are real people. The more you can make those illusions seem real, the more chances you have of your reader being transported from their daily life into the world you have created. Your goal is to take your reader away from the real world that they reside in to the fictional world that you have created. As an author, you want your reader to feel that your characters are substantial, authentic and dimensional. In the following pages we'll cover the process for making this happen. When you're finished reading it, you'll be able to make a real person out of all the characters you choose to create.

Alright now, that was enough talk. Now it's time to get down to business. The first thing you need to know about creating characters is that they have to possess two things: Desire and individuality. If you really want to create a realistic character, you'll have to give him or her these two-character traits.

DESIRE: All of your main characters should have some kind of desire. They have to want something. Desire is the driving force of all people and a well written character can keep your urban novel moving forward. The idea of showing and not telling holds true to characters as well. If you create a protagonist who has a big heart and cares about his family, all while having a perfect home life, your readers will get bored really fast and eventually put your book down. But they won't get bored if you have that same character receive a phone call telling him that his mother has suddenly disappeared and is most likely on a drug binge like in the story *Money iz the Motive* by Mike Enemigo and Ca$ciou$ Green. That phone call forced him to round up all his homies to help find his mother which ended up causing more problems after he finds the man who was feeding her the drugs and he kills him.

It's good for your character to have a desire that can become the difference between life or death. However, it doesn't always have to be like that. Your protagonist can have something that is simple for his desire, but if he wants it bad enough, it can drive a major plot forward. For instance, if your main character found a purse that belonged to a beautiful woman and he wants to meet her, it's not life or death hanging in the air; but your reader will care just as long as your character wants it bad enough. That's the benefit of having a character with desire. The plot will grow from his need to have what he wants. If your protagonist is willing to go to the ends of the earth to deliver that purse, then there's all kinds of possibilities of where that story can go.

INDIVIDUALITY: Nothing makes a story more boring

than a character who acts like a million other people. When you look at stereotypes and try to create a character to fit those stereotypes, you kill the story. How many times have you read a book, or watched a movie that had an Asian store owner who says with an accent: "You buy or get out!" Or, what about the pimp who beats his hoes and makes them call him Daddy?

Let's try switching this up a lil' bit. What if you make that old foreign store owner the head of the Asian Mafia? So, when your protagonist enters the store and disrespects him, all kinds of things start to happen. Or, can you imagine a pimp who really wants to help his ho-bitches accomplish something with their lives? Such distinctiveness separates these characters from all the other ones who fall into stereotypical categories. This is what is going to make your urban novel stand apart from the rest. These gems are what will create dimension and individuality for these characters; and that's exactly what you want.

Since we're covering stereotypes, then we should also talk about the simple mistake a lot of writers commit when they create their characters. When you create an evil character, he shouldn't be 100% evil. If you want to give your characters dimension, they can't be all good or all bad. If you've built up a protagonist who is a nun that has dedicated her life to her parishes and the church comes into a problem with money, she can go around asking for donations just like any other nun in her position would. But what if she comes up with a once in a lifetime scheme to pull off a multimillion-dollar lick? That would definitely give this nun some dimension, right?

This is how you create a complex character. This is also how you create a realistic character. In real life, no one is 100% good all the time. No one is perfect. So, this allows your readers to empathize with your characters. The same goes for your evil characters as well. A great way to surprise your reader is by having an evil character do something that is out of the ordinary at a major turning point of your story.

The trick to this is that throughout your story you would have to hint and build up to this certain character trait; this way, when it happens, your readers will come to their own conclusions that say: "You know what, that makes sense..."

It won't work if your reader doesn't believe it. Therefore, it's up to you to introduce your characters to your readers in a way so that they will see the inside of your character's emotions. Nothing is worse than having your reader walk away from your urban novel thinking there's no way in hell that character would've handled that situation like that.

The following is an excerpt out of my book *How To Hustle & Win: Sex, Money, Murder Edition*. In the chapter where this came from, I humanize myself to the point where anyone who has ever really experienced The Game could relate to the realness of my plight...

... At the Greyhound station, I bought a ticket to Chattanooga. (I told y'all about Eddie.) While I was waiting for the bus to load, I noticed a woman with two young children getting ready to get on the same bus as me. I was going through the motions of leaving my pregnant wife, which was an emotional feat within itself. She didn't want me to leave; she was crying and pleading for me to stay. As I think back on it now, I realize her tears were coming from an innocent love that only comes once in a lifetime. If she only knew the pain I would cause her just a few moments later, she probably would have turned around and never looked back.

When the bus finally departed, I sat back thinking of what the future had in store for me. After a while, I did a quick perimeter check and realized that baby with the two kids was seated next to me. It didn't take long for me to start a conversation. When I did, I found out that she was also leaving an old life for a new one. Just like me. She was leaving a violent relationship and heading to Oklahoma. I was leaving a violent lifestyle and heading to Tennessee.

Over the next few days, we sat next to one another and

ended up getting kind of close. I told her about the brother I'd never met, in Tennessee. How I felt as if my whole life had been a training exercise for the mission I had ahead of me. I was excited, yet at the same time, nervous from the unexpected. When the time came for us to part ways, I could see that something was bothering her. We had become close enough for me to ask what was wrong, and what she said stuck with me for the rest of my life. She said that she was sad for me. That when she looked into my eyes, she didn't see pain, she didn't see suffering, and she didn't see malignancy. I told her I didn't understand what she was trying to say, so she went on to tell me that people in The Game have a certain look in their eyes. She said that if the things I told her about my brother were true, then she was sure I'd see what she was talking about once I took a gander into his eyes. What made her so sad was that my eyes didn't have that look. However, she felt that if she was to see me a few years down the road, I would have that look. God... that lady was so right!

Whenever I think of that day, I wish I would have listened to her. I still wish I could one day speak to her again. And you know what? I don't think we'd have to actually talk. I know if she were to see me again, my eyes would tell it all.

At the time, I felt like she was telling me that I was lacking something. I felt slighted and I told her that she had me mixed up with someone else! By that time in my life, I had already sold a good amount of narcotics, shot several people, and served four years in the California Youth Authority. I thought she was saying/implying that I was soft or weak. But that wasn't the case. She told me that I would only understand what she was trying to tell me the day I woke up, looked in the mirror and realized that something had changed. I knew what she was talking about; I had already seen it before. What was so cold about the situation was that I wanted what she was construing. I was a young gangsta and I wanted the world to know it. I made an effort to show the world that I was an outlaw. I didn't give a damn what anyone thought about it...

CAN YOUR CHARACTERS CHANGE?

Earlier while writing about plots, I mentioned the fact that characters can change throughout a story, and that sometimes makes a story more believable. The thing is, your reader should see the potential for change. In *Money iz the Motive*, Kano (the protagonist of the story) goes to prison at an early age. The thing is, Ca$ciou$ Green, the author, established early on in the story that Kano was extremely intelligent.

So as the story went on, it was actually believable that Kano would've went to prison and listened to his elders. If a character's desire is the drive of the story and in the process he changes, it becomes the story's culmination. However, just because the potential for your character to change is there, it doesn't mean that your character should change. The thing is, when a character is going through life without the chance to better himself, or worsen himself, the story becomes predictable.

WHERE DID THIS GUY COME FROM?

To create a memorable character who your readers will care about you'll need a starting point. Where is your boy from? What made him into the person he is today? If you sit back and think about all the people you've met throughout your life, you'll have ideas for characters flowing uncontrollably from your fingertips.

A lot of writers start characters from the memory of an interesting person they've met throughout their lives. Some even base characters on themselves. The latter actually happens quite often in urban novels. Starting a character from people you know gives you a strong sense of intimacy. This will allow you to create a believable and realistic character.

The catch is, when you're creating a character from a real person you need to leave room for creativity. Once you incorporate a character into your urban novel you should keep in mind that you're writing an urban novel. You shouldn't have to limit all the character's decisions to reality. You can, and you should, transform these characters to suit your needs.

You can also create characters from people you don't know. Let's say you drove by a crossing guard. It's a great idea to try and imagine what kind of story can emerge from this crossing guard. Real quick, I can think of one right now where a violent hit and run occurred where he witnessed it and now the driver behind the wheel of the car who hit someone is trying to kill him so he won't be able to testify against him. Or, what if you see a prison transport bus pass by? There can be all kinds of stories you can come up with from any one of the convicts on that bus. Characters can come from anywhere at any time. All you have to do is look for 'em.

Some people say that the greatest feat of a writer who has created a character is his ability to think inside of that character's head. When you've accomplished this that means you've finally succeeded in creating a real person. If you can do this then the rest can go on cruise control. That character will control his or her own destiny. That's when you know that your character is fully awake; when they begin to make their own decisions.

When you are in the process of creating your character, you should push to create him into a four-dimensional person. These dimensions include appearance, history, personality and self-identity.

APPEARANCE is the first dimension. You don't want to create a physical stereotype and then be stuck with it your whole story. But then again, the way a person looks does tell a lot about that person. From the type of clothes they wear to their style of hair, these details tell you a lot about a person when you initially see them walking up the street. The way a person looks also tells tons about their attitude and personality.

HISTORY is the second dimension. Knowing that a specific drug dealer grew up in a single-child home, and was spoiled as a child, can tell your reader multitudes about your character. This person would definitely be different than the average hustler who grew up in a broken home and had to fight for everything he's ever had.

PERSONALITY is the third dimension and it falls back on the first two: appearance and past. The personality is basically what your character is really like. Is he insecure? Does he have a chip on his shoulder? Is he narcissistic and spoiled? Or, does he view the world as a giant crab bucket where he's gotta do whatever it takes to survive in such a harsh reality? Your character's personality will dictate a large part of the story. It's what will help him make the decisions when certain situations fall in his or her path.

SELF IDENTITY is the fourth dimension and you mustn't get it mixed up with the last one. This is how your character views himself. Since we've been talking about a drug dealer, I'll use that persona as an example. There are some individuals in the game who view themselves as business men, then there's the ones who consider themselves to be gangsters. Who does your character see himself as? Does his self-perception match his history? Does it match his appearance?

Here's a guideline you can use for when you're creating a four-dimensional character:

A good tool to use while creating a character is to build a profile. The way you do this is by making a file on your characters that will enable you to understand them better. I can help you by giving you a list of questions you can ask yourself about all of your characters. If you fill out a sort of questionnaire with the following questions, you'll have a strong profile to go by.

1. What's your character's handle? What do people call him or her?
2. What's his/her hair and eye color?
3. Does he have any scars, tattoos or birthmarks? When did he get 'em?
4. Where is your character from? Was he born there?
5. Is there a private place he goes to alleviate stress?
6. Does your character have any fears? Is there anyone close enough to him to know it as well?
7. Is there a secret he or she is hiding from the rest of the world?
8. Has your character ever been in love; is he in love now?

All these details we're working on now is for your main character. Most urban novels have many different characters, but not all of them should be built up to this level. If they are, you run the risk of confusing your readers. It doesn't really matter if the smaller characters have ever been in love, or likes red shoes, does it? Your secondary characters might need some building up, but not as much as your protagonist. The only other person who needs as much building as the protagonist is the antagonist. When you have two main characters pitted against each other it makes your story deeper. But only if your readers understand who they both really are.

MINOR CHARACTERS

Minor characters are the other characters who will populate your story. However, their roles are limited so you don't have to spend as much time building them up because it doesn't really matter. If you spend too much time building up a minor character you can confuse the reader by making him think that he should pay attention to this person. We really don't need to know any intimate details about the pretty waitress at the truck stop where your character stopped on his way out of state, do we?

Here're a few notes to keep in mind when you're creating minor characters.

1. Watch your stereotyping. Stereotyping is real tempting to an author when creating minor characters because these characters don't play a big role in the story. Especially since you only have a few sentences to describe them in. It's best to use your personal experiences to help in describing these people.

2. If the minor character is going to make more than one appearance then their first appearance should be memorable. If not, when they show up later, your reader won't remember them.

3. Give your minor characters interesting names, but not too close to any of the main characters. This is a common mistake writer make and it confuses the reader. Try staying away from average names because that might confuse your readers as well.

4. Keep in mind that even though these characters don't play a large part in your story they will certainly add depth to certain elements of your urban novel.

PAINTING PICTURES WITH WORDS

Now, remember, when writing an urban novel you're trying to paint a picture with words; a picture that moves, so it's better to show than tell. There are four more ways to show your reader who your character really is and that's by action, speech, appearance and thought. If you're able to describe these four aspects of your character it will bring understanding to your reader on a deeper level.

Here they go:

ACTION. The way your character acts in a crisis will show the inner person of that character. He can act and look like a gangsta, but if he gets to blabbin' when the police come around asking questions, then your reader can come to their own conclusion that he's a sucka.

SPEECH. The way a person looks and acts can tell a lot about that person, but the way your character speaks can tell where a person is from or what level of education a person has. Speech can even tell you if a person respects the person he or she is talking to.

APPEARANCE. The appearance a person keeps up can tell you a lot about that person's character. What about their facial expressions? Does your character smile when he meets a new person? Is he a shifty person who doesn't like to look at people in their eyes when he speaks to them? Does he saw his skinny jeans and wear do-rags, or does he sport button-ups and slacks?

SELF IDENTITY. You know, you can actually use thought to show a character's self-perception. We'll go into it a lot deeper at a later point, but keep it in mind. Using thought will tell your reader a lot about your character without having him say anything out loud.

These are just four tools that allow you to show who your characters are instead of telling your reader who they are. When you take your time and do it right, it will add seasoning to an already tasty plate of soul food.

TEN GEMS

1. All of your main characters should have some kind of desire.

2. Creating individuality in your characters will make your urban novel stand out from the rest.

3. None of your characters should be all good or all bad all the time.

4. Characters can change throughout a story and sometimes this is what will make your story more believable.

5. To create a memorable character, your readers will need a starting point. Give them a backstory on your character.

6. The greatest feat of a writer is his ability to think inside the head of the character who he has created.

7. A four-dimensional character includes appearance, history, personality and self-identity.

8. A good tool to use while creating a character is to build a profile.

9. Don't spend too much time building up minor characters.

10. Four ways to "show" your reader who your characters are is: Action; Speech; Appearance; Thought.

CHAPTER TEN

Dialogue

Have you ever saw someone from a distance who you suddenly decided you wanted to hook up with? Then, after you step to 'em and that person opened his or her mouth, you found out that she wasn't the person who you assumed she'd be? I've found myself in that situation on several occasions on both ends of that spectrum. I remember a couple of times when a female has approached me and all I had to do was keep my mouth shut and we'd be leaving the club together, then I'd say something idiotic and end up leaving the club solo. I've also chased after some bad females just to find out that I couldn't even hold a decent conversation with 'em.

Urban novels can create that same feeling if someone picks it up expecting to be entertained and they end up getting bored. You can look at it like a date. When your reader opens your book, they picked it up because there was something about that book that made them want to spend some time in its world. And that's where we come into the subject of dialogue. You can try to write an urban novel without dialogue, but it won't work. Going back to the "date" analogy, how many dates have you been on without an exchange of words? It wouldn't work because dialogue is how people communicate.

And just like in real life, your readers want to see your

characters interacting with one another. That's what they came for. It's one thing for an author to show and tell a story, but readers want to watch the characters come to life. Dialogue is what gives them a life of their own. Isn't making your people come alive why you created them in the first place?

In case you need more explanation on what dialogue is, everything in an urban novel that isn't narration is considered dialogue. Dialogue is what your characters say. There is no set limit on how much dialogue there should be in each story. Yet, most writers find a balance between narration and dialogue. Your story will go a lot smoother when you learn to switch back and forth between the two. Because dialogue can move a story along really quickly, it's a good tool to utilize.

SCENE OR SUMMARY?

Two of the most fundamental ways to reveal any moment in your story is through scene and summary. A summary is when you explain a scene. A scene is when you use dialogue to show and tell your reader what is happening; like a soap opera. You're gonna use both techniques when writing your urban novel. However, showing is always better than telling, so there will be times when it will be more intriguing to use scene instead of summary. Summary is best used when you're trying to move the story along quickly towards the next scene.

Basically, you're not gonna get very far in the world of urban novels if you don't learn how to write dialogue properly. You can have a great idea, and an interesting plot in your story, but if your dialogue is wack it's gonna destroy all the other work you've put in on it.

Here's a few techniques to keep in mind while you're creating dialogue between your characters:

1. Don't think; just go! Later on, we'll talk about revision. I'll explain how the first and second drafts of your book aren't supposed to be perfect. You have to learn to just write. Let it all out. When you first start writing a scene with dialogue, just write, don't worry about spelling, or quotations, or who is saying what. Write the whole exchange in paragraph form and come back later to shine it all up.

After you finally get it all down, you can go back and separate who from what and add and take out. This way your options will be wider. You'll have a chance to come up with a more realistic exchange. This really works, just try it and see what I'm talking about for yourself.

2. Avoid the echoes. A common mistake beginners make when creating dialogue is wasting time and space with a back and forth exchange that does nothing to move the story along. I call it echoes because that's exactly what it is. Here's an example:

"Yo, son," asked Drake.

"What's good, son?" replied Eazy.

"Nada, just gettin' this bread, what about you?"

"Man, I'm just posted up, what's good?"

"I need to talk to you."

"Well, what's up? Let's talk."

That's the kind of dialogue I'm talking about. It'll kill your book. Don't do it like that. Avoid it at all cost. Now I'm gonna give you an example on how to move your story along more realistically and avoid the echoes in the process, all while using the same line of dialogue.

"Yo, son."

"Where you been?" asked Eazy.

"Man, I'm out here getting this paper, but something came up and we need to talk," replied Drake.

"Alright, but come sit in my car. I don't want these dudes in our business."

Now this exchange tells us so much more than the first one. The first clue is one of your characters asks the other one where he's been. That tells the reader that both guys know each other, but the visitor obviously hasn't been around for a while. Then the other one tells him to get in the car, and that tells us that he expects the conversation to be explicit. It also shows that he doesn't trust the other hustler's on the block with that information. Why should he expect the conversation to be explicit; where has the visitor been? How do they know each other? These are just a few of the points that come from this exchange and it automatically made this conversation more realistic than the first time around.

3. Silence please. Yes, you can utilize silence while writing dialogue. Silence can sometimes tell your reader something more intimate than direct dialogue can. I'm gonna continue to use the original dialogue we've been working on, but this time I'm gonna use the silence technique to juice it up a lil'.

"Yo, son."

"Man, where you been, Drake?"

"I've been out here gettin' it, but something came up and we need to talk."

They both stared at one another, exchanging a look that only two lifelong friends would understand.

"Alright," replied Eazy." But come sit in my car. I don't want these dudes up in our business."

See how moments of silence added more to that exchange than the first and second time around? If I wanted to, I could've changed the wording around some more as well. This is all part of the magic of dialogue. If you learn how to sharpen these skills your urban novel will become a classic.

4. Shine up your work. You can always go back and change your original ideas. That's what's cool about writing urban novels; you can remix fact with fiction. I remember an

incident in Tampa when I was at a club and I decided to approach a group of females on the dance floor. When I reached their group it seemed like they tightened their circle, refusing to let me get anywhere near the inside of their private party. I was drunk and I know I looked like a damn fool standing there on the outside of their circle. I was pretty mad that night, but at least now I can look back on that incident and laugh about it. But you know I love writing urban novels because I can take that incident and add it into any of my stories and switch up the details to my likening. Now, instead of just standing there looking stupid, I would take three of those girls home with me.

That's what writing fiction is all about. Just because it starts out a certain way in real life, doesn't mean it has to stay that way. Shine it up like some brand-new rims.

5. Add some talk-show-shit to your work. If you look around close enough, you'll start recognizing that billions of dollars are made every year from selling drama. Why do you think there are so many reality TV shows? You can get a piece of that pie by adding confrontation to your dialogue and by giving your plot a back-story.

Here, I'll show you what I'm talking about with the dialogue we've already started on:

Drake walked up to the spot that he and his longtime friend, Eazy, helped establish. Eazy was grinding, but Drake had been missing in action for the last few weeks. During that time he met a female that happened to have in her possession a nice amount of stolen heroin. The problem was that the work belonged to Drake and Eazy's connect. And their connect, Carlos, had already put the word out on the street that he was willing to pay top dollar for that female's head. Nevertheless, Drake had been helping her hide out and sell the work she had stolen from Carlos. The two friends hadn't had a chance to speak to each other in weeks, but Eazy had heard rumors saying certain things that he hoped weren't true. But now that Drake had suddenly shown up, Eazy had a feeling that he was about to find out the rumors were true.

(With this backstory, let's continue with the dialogue.)

"Yo, son."

"Where you been, fam?"

"Man, I've been gettin' it, but something came up and we need to talk."

They both stared at each other, exchanging a look that only two lifelong friends would understand.

"Alright, Drake, but first let's get in the whip, I don't want these dudes in our mix."

They both stepped into Eazy's Buick Lesabre and a long silence ensued. Both men knew that whatever came of this conversation would most likely be life altering. The word on the streets said that Drake had gotten his hands on some pure heroin and there were even quitter whispers saying that he was fucking the bitch who had stolen the dope.

"You already know what it is, Eazy. It's our time."

Eazy was half expecting this conversation for a while now. However, until that exact moment he hadn't made up his mind about what he would say. "Drake, you wildin'. I can't ride wit' you this time. You know I got a shorty now. I can't take risks like this."

"Man, when you killed that sucka on 43rd and we had to go to war over your punk-ass baby mamma, I didn't say shit! I lost everything I had! Now I'm coming to you and you're gonna tell me you ain't got my back?!"

Eazy couldn't look his friend in the eyes. He dropped his stare to his palms, thinking about all the times he asked his friend for help, never once being turned away. He also thought about how long it had taken to cultivate a relationship of that caliber. On top of that, he knew what stakes were up in the air. If the rumors were true, which this conversation meant they were, then Drake was sitting on over a million dollars of heroin. Whatever he decided next would most likely determine the course of the rest of his life.

Eazy looked into Drake's eyes and said, "I hope you got a plan..."

Now, think about that original piece of dialogue we started with a few pages back and how it turned into what you just read. I utilized silence, thought, gave a lil' backstory and added drama. The outcome was pretty interesting if you ask me. That's what dialogue can add to your story. That was a real-life exchange between two lifelong friends. The cold thing about all this is that Drake and Eazy aren't even real people.

That was fun and it worked, but you want to make sure you don't use dialogue on scenes that don't need it. You should save your dialogue for scenes in your urban novel that hold real significance to your story. Nobody wants to sit through a conversation between two old ladies when the two main characters in your story just agreed to go to war with the local drug syndicate.

If the scene is important to your story, your reader wants to be there. This is why urban novel enthusiasts open these books in the first place. So, give it to 'em. Don't make them accompany some old lady on a trip to the grocery store. That ain't cool.

The best way to learn how to write realistic dialogue is by listening to real dialogue. In your real everyday life, you'll always be around people who are talking on cell phones, to their kids, friends or store clerks. All you have to do is sit back and listen. It'll payoff when it's time for you to write some dialogue for your book.

The only problem with taking notes from real conversations is that urban novel readers expect a little more from your dialogue than they do in real life. Your dialogue needs to have more impact, focus and relevance than a normal conversation. You're gonna have to portray the tension and reality of each situation to your reader through words on paper. Ergo, you'll need skill and it's not always as easy as it sounds.

It helps to add physical action to all of your dialogue scenes as well. When real people talk to each other they don't just sit there motionless. Some people talk with their hands. In a car, you might be holding a conversation while you're searching through your pockets for your keys. If you add these images to your dialogue scenes, you'll be creating a picture that seems more real to your reader.

If you don't show your readers what the characters in your story are doing, it becomes a report that they are grading instead of a world they've entered and became part of.

By adding narration to your dialogue, you are giving your scene a real physical presence. That's what is going to separate your work from the writings of an amateur.

INDIRECT DIALOGUE

Earlier, when I mentioned summary, I forgot to tell you that you can also summarize dialogue, too. This is called indirect dialogue. It's when you tell your reader what was said instead of having them sit through the whole conversation. Indirect dialogue needs to come at the right moment, when the weight of the situation is more important than the actual conversation itself.

For an example I'll use the same characters we've already been working with so far.

In this scene, Eazy is explaining to Drake that the Feds are on to them. They just pulled him over and shook him down:

Drake tried to calm his homey down, but there was no slowing down his rant. Eazy was pacing across the room while waving his arms as he explained what had just taken place.

"They pulled me out the whip! All ski-masked up and shit! Bruh, they got some way-out intel. Talking 'bout, 'Where's your boy Drake? We know you guys killed Herm and Loc. Where's all the heroin? You guys are going down'. I yada yada yada! These mothafuckas' is on us, bruh!"

By summarizing the incident, you get the most important information out of the situation. Sometimes the reader doesn't have to sit through the whole back and forth between every situation, but at least this way the information is out in the open. The FEDS know about the drugs and the murders, so what's gonna happen next? I didn't even write a story to go along with all this dialogue I just created, but now I'm wondering what's gonna happen next. That's the magic of dialogue!

Dialogue also helps build characters. Just like when I told y'all how I lost a few potential conquests by opening my mouth and spitting some ignorant shit. It can happen in your stories, too. Your character can easily approach a female in the club and when he reaches her, he's greeted by a foul-mouthed alcoholic tramp. That's a realistic situation and if you mention how fine she was, it'll surprise your readers. It'll show them that appearance can tell you a lot about a person, but dialogue will show you even more.

Always keep in mind that everyone is unique in their own special way. Not everyone speaks the same way, especially if they are from different states. If you have all your characters speaking the same way you'll be taking away from their individuality.

Another trick to the trade that you should capitalize on is miscommunication. Miscommunication adds tension to the scene. It also gives the reader an inside knowledge of what's going on when the characters don't even know. Have you ever watched a scary movie and yelled at the person on the screen, telling them not to open the door that the killer is standing behind? Well, that's the same feeling that you can give to your readers if you learn to capitalize on miscommunications.

Curse words: You're most likely gonna use bad language at one time or another, especially when writing an urban novel. The truth of the matter is that you have to at one time or another if you want your dialog to sound realistic. The thing is, when you write course language and your reader reads it, it doesn't go over as quickly as it would have in real life. It also exposes the author of the story in an unnecessary way. I try to dodge curse words as much as possible. Nevertheless, they do come out every once in a while. Profanity is more vulgar on paper than in real life, so keep that in mind and use them sparsely.

I can only imagine how many of you will go on to create classics after reading this book. I'm really lacing you with some priceless gems. All you have to do is internalize this knowledge and it'll start to automatically flow out whenever you sit down to write. You'll see.

THE GEMS

1. Every urban novel needs dialogue. It's what brings the story to life.
2. The two most fundamental ways to reveal any moment in your story is through scene or summary.
3. Summary is best used when you are trying to move the story along quickly.
4. Avoid echoes.
5. Utilize silence and thought.
6. Add drama by giving your plot a back story.
7. Avoid using dialogue on scenes that aren't important.
8. It always helps to add physical action to your dialogue.
9. Summarizing dialogue should come when the weight of the situation is more important than the actual conversation.
10. Miscommunication adds tension to a scene. It also gives the reader an inside knowledge of what is going on when the characters don't.

CHAPTER ELEVEN

Point of View

In college I took a criminal justice course where the teacher, an ex-pig, gave us a quiz. He had a fellow teacher come into the class wearing a hoody while carrying a toy gun. This hooded character then robbed the class. Of course, we were prepped on what was going to happen before it happened, but the actual robbery wasn't the point of the exercise. Afterwards, our teacher told the whole class to write a detailed report describing the crime that was committed.

Over the following week the teacher read each report out loud to the whole class, and a funny thing happened. Not one single report gave the same account of the crime. Even though there was only one incident, there were twenty students who witnessed it, so that meant that there was twenty different points of view. That's something that happens in real life all the time. One of the biggest decisions you'll have to make when writing you're urban novel is which point of view you're gonna give to the world.

The p.o.v. you choose for your story will dictate how your readers will react emotionally to your characters and their actions. It's also going to affect the tone and theme of your work. We haven't covered "theme" yet, but when we do, all the pieces are gonna fit together. So, it's important that you recognize the importance of choosing the correct point of view to tell your story from.

FIRST PERSON POINT OF VIEW

When you tell a story from the first-person narrative your story is going to be told by a character in the story. Usually, in first person p.o.v., it's the main character telling the story. The protagonist is telling the reader what he does throughout the novel. Most novice urban novel writers who base their stories on real life tend to use this p.o.v. They do this because their story is usually biographical in nature.

Stories that are told in first person must remain in the character's voice throughout the whole urban novel. If the protagonist is a Jamaican drug lord, you'll have to narrate the whole story through the voice and eyes of this character.

In first parson narrative the character telling the story can actually address the reader. While he's telling the story, he can turn to the readers and give them his thoughts on what just took place. He can even ask them questions. The feeling you're trying to create is that the narrator is telling his story while he's sitting right next to the reader.

Here's an excerpt out of my book *How to Hustle & Win: Sex, Money, Murder Edition*, a book I wrote in first person POV...

War is just as much a part of The Game as money. At one point or another, you will find yourself in a situation where guns will be needed and people will die. You might have a good run for a while, but if you're in The Game for an ample amount of time, it will happen: War is inevitable.

To me, war is serious business. It's when you can feel death knocking at your door, or hiding in the shadows. It's when you're forced to put all of your leisure activities on hold. When you have to ship the wifey and kids out of town for a few weeks. War is when you're pitted against an opponent who is just as dangerous as you and you know it. That's war.

I've been called to about three different tours of duty throughout my life. If you've lived the street/gang life, chances are you've shot at someone or been shot at. You might even have a catalog of war stories to tell about nights when bullets have ricocheted off cars and/or walls. But just because you've been in a few shoot-outs doesn't mean you've actually been in a war. You can always tell who's really experienced war, because those are the guys who don't want to do it again. Yeah, a true warrior will go to battle time and time again if called for, but he knows the seriousness of it, so he doesn't go looking for it.

You'll know when you're really at war because people die. The people closest to you are the ones who tend to get it. And it usually takes several months to come to fruition. Both sides take loses and most of the time there's no clear winner.

I've got a long history of shooting people. I've carried guns from a young age, but my involvement in what I consider a real war didn't take place until I was released from the California Youth Authority. I was so eager to prove myself that I always jumped at the chance to ride. I volunteered for every drive-by or ambush the big homies organized. We were feuding with a set of Crips that hung out at Rainbow Park in South Sacramento. At times, tit-for-tats (back-n-forth shoot-outs and ambushes) took place two or three times in one night.

In the end, there weren't any clear winners or losers. I didn't care, though. I got to prove myself and that's all that mattered. It didn't even bother me when I found out it all started over a bitch. Ali, the homey, had gone out of bounds to meet up with a hoodrat from the other side and got himself shot....

One of the main advantages of telling a story in first person p.o.v. is that the writer can become intimate with the reader. He can give him a specific view from the eyes of the person who actually experienced the story. It's a great way of getting your reader involved on an intimate level.

There are some problems that come with first person p.o.v., though. Now you're stuck in the viewpoint of that one character. If one of the characters in your urban novel is telling your reader the story through his point of view, he can't possibly know what another character is thinking. You're also limited because if your protagonist wasn't there when something goes down, he can only tell your reader what he heard happened; not what he saw, since he wasn't there to see it go down. You'll also have to tell the story with a vocabulary and intelligence of that character. If your main character is an ignorant old man, you'll have to stay in that suit throughout the whole story. Are you ready to tackle a mission like that?

FIRST PERSON-MULTIPLE VIEWS

I've read a few urban novels that were written in multiple first persons, and truthfully, I tend to get confused at first. I think the reason I get confused so much is because it takes a minute for me to realize how what I'm reading was written. I'll go into the book thinking it was written a certain way and I'll get lost in translation. But once I get used to the style most of these stories end up being pretty cool.

What I do like about multiple view, first person narratives is that the reader gets more than one point of view to the story. Sometimes there's two character that are completely opposite, but they're on the same team. Like in the movie "Belly" with Nas and DMX. That movie was narrated by Nas, but if it was done in multiple-view, first-person p.o.v. we would've seen the story unfold through the eyes of DMX also. X and Nas were hustling together in that movie. However, if your urban novel has an interesting antagonist, it might make a good story to see it unfold through the eyes of that character as well as the protagonist.

Some multiple, first person narratives are done in a way that each character gets his or her own chapter when giving their p.o.v. Other authors leave extra space between paragraphs when the characters change, but that will confuse some of your readers. One of the best things about multipe person point of view is that it engages the reader a lot more than single person p.o.v. In multiple person the reader gets several different p.o.v.'s so he can decide for himself who he wants to side with. This can become an interesting experience for the reader, and can set your book apart from other styles of urban novels.

FIRST PERSON PERIPHERAL

Most of the stories that are written in first person p.o.v. are narrated by the main character of the story. This isn't the case when you're writing from a peripheral point of view. The narrator is a whole other person in the story. The peripheral p.o.v. is most effective when the actions of the main character have a profound effect on another person or group of people.

A good example is a love story when one of the two characters who are in love have a best friend or a pet. Yeah ... a pet! Since you're telling the story from a "bystander's" point of view, what's stopping you from letting the pit bull tell the story?

The flaw in the p.o.v. is that the narrator has to stay in the body of that bystander. Sometimes the bystander has to leave, or just isn't there when one of the protagonists has to leave. So you'll be stuck summarizing a lot of scenes since you should never deviate from your p.o.v.

THIRD PERSON SINGLE-VISION

When you decide to write in third person, the story isn't gonna be told by a character in your story. In this style you'll be telling your reader everything about everyone in your urban novel. You can see everything and you know the thoughts of all your characters. In this p.o.v. the narrator knows all the past, present and future of all the characters. He also has the power to give the reader any and all the information he wants, whenever he wants to.

In all the other p.o.v.'s the reader is fed limited information from different characters. But through third person narrative, all the 411 is given from a narrator who knows "all." Through this power you have the ability to enter the mind of any, or all of the characters in your story. You can explain any event that takes place in your urban novel from firsthand knowledge. You can describe incidents experienced, or thought of, by any and all characters. You can provide historical context or future events for your reader.

This style gives you the most freedom. Instead of being limited by the wisdom and intelligence of a made-up character you can tell the story from an "all-seeing" point of view. This doesn't mean you have to give the voice of your narrator a god-like presence. You can give him his own unique voice, but we'll cover that later in another chapter.

You can also use third person narrative to add suspense to your urban novel. Just because you know what's gonna happen next doesn't mean your characters know. If you're writing an urban novel where there's a robbery scene and several characters are gonna die, you can easily tell your reader that only 3 out of 5 of the gang is gonna make it home alive. That'll keep your reader turning pages. Now he'll want to know who will make it and who won't. Of course, none of the characters know what's about to happen so they'll be walking into that situation like Stevie Wonder. Suspense at its finest.

The reason a lot of writers decide to use this style of p.o.v is because it reminds the reader of the author. It's not as realistic for the reader as it is hearing the story through the eyes of one of the characters. This can cost intimacy and empathy your reader could have accumulated for any specific character.

$$$$$

Regardless of which p.o.v. you choose in writing any of your urban novels, you have to realize that once you begin a story in a specific p.o.v. you have to stick with it. If you step away from your chosen p.o.v. you're not only risking that your reader will get confused, but you will also distract him from the story you've been creating. An easy way to make sure you don't go off path with this rule is to go through your manuscript paragraph by paragraph to make sure you didn't slip up.

You must pick which point of view you'll be writing your urban novel room before you embark on writing your story. Sometimes your first choice isn't always the best one.

Here's a list of questions to ask yourself that will help you with your choice:

1. Who will be affected the most by your story? Will someone in your urban novel be emotionally involved in most of the plot? Sometimes, that is the best person to narrate your story because it will allow your reader to become up close and personal with the character most affected by your story.

2. Who is gonna be there when your urban novel reaches its climax? Remember, you'll be giving your reader an account of what happens through the eyes of the narrator, so this narrator should be there when the shit hits the fan, don't you think?

3. Who is around the most? Your reader wants to be there inside the story. Is there someone inside your story that's always around, and can have firsthand knowledge to lace your readers with?

4. Is there anyone interesting enough to tell the story? You're the person who creates the characters, and sometimes

you'll have a character that's so funny that he sees the world through an interesting set of eyes. Your readers might enjoy listening to this character's antics. You can also look at it like this; the narrator is the person driving a tour bus through your world. Who do you want as your tour guide?

No matter which p.o.v. you choose, always keep in mind that your goal is to give your reader a page-turning urban novel. One that will leave them wanting more of your work. You want the reader to close your book with an experience that he or she will never forget.

TEN GEMS

1. Point of view is whose eyes your reader will see the action from.
2. First person narrative is when a character in your story tells the story.
3. In first person narrative the narrator can speak to the reader.
4. First-person multiple views is when the story is being told by several different characters.
5. In multiple person narrative the reader can decide who to side with throughout the story.
6. First-person peripheral is when the secondary character is the narrator of the story.
7. Based on the fact that it's not the main character who is telling the story there will be a lot of summarizing because the narrator won't always be there.
8. Third person narrative is when the story isn't being told by someone in the story.
9. Third person narrative can be used to add extra suspense to your urban novel because you can talk to your readers about things that your characters don't know about.
10. No matter what you do, do not deviate from the point of view you're telling your story from.

CHAPTER TWELVE

Descriptions

I keep saying that the goal in writing urban novels is to create a story where your reader is able to leave his daily grind and enter the world you've manufactured. In order for you to accomplish this goal you are going to need to stimulate your reader's senses. The world you create has to seem real, so real that they can feel it, hear it, see it and taste it. This is called "sensual writing." In sensual writing, you create a story where your reader doesn't just watch a character in your urban novel, he enters his body. If your character is afraid then your reader should be scared.

If your character is filled with adrenaline your reader should feel the rush. Sensual writing opens the door for your reader to step into the passenger seat of your protagonist's vehicle. This is the only way that your reader is going to be able to leave the drudgery of his daily life and enter the world you have created.

SYNESTHESIA

Most sense descriptions can't be described. If you try you'll run the risk of sounding elementary and dry. The best way to describe a sense is to use what is called synesthesia. Synesthesia is the act of using one sense to describe another. And it takes skill.

Let's say you want to describe a taste, if you use synesthesia, you'll use other senses like smells, sounds and visuals. Something like this:

When Eazy finally sat down to eat his T-bone steak he couldn't wait to sink his teeth into the roasted meat. Every time he ate a steak from this restaurant, he felt like he was sitting on a yacht, floating down the French Riviera. Chewing on that meat was like watching the beautiful sun setting over a faraway ocean.

This description of taste takes the reader to a whole different setting. It allows the reader to enter the mind of the character and see what he sees while he is enjoying that steak. This is what synesthesia is all about, using senses to describe a scene.

MEMORY

Describing memory is purely psychological. In real life, a memory can be triggered by all kinds of senses. If you put a song into your MP3 player, depending on your experience with that song it can take you back to another era. That's what Lil Wayne's Carter 4 does for me. Usher and R Kelly can trigger memories of youthful love for millions of people who used to listen to that music while making slow love to their first love.

Here's a scene I'd use to bring a memory into a story:

Lacy and her mother were walking along Pier 89, at Fisherman's Wharf in San Francisco when she noticed her mother pause while strolling in front of a sidewalk restaurant that served clam chowder. It all happened so fast that she just shrugged it off not knowing that the smell of the ocean mixed with the aroma of clam chowder had taken her mother to another place and time in her life. A time filled with love and trust on the New England shoreline, where she had first met Lacy's father...

TOUCH

The sense of touch is the richest sense of information there is for human stimuli. Touch is pain and pleasure. Pain can be pleasure and pleasure can sometimes be considered taboo. If you can describe the sense of physically touching something, you are on your way to inviting your reader inside your character's "car". It helps to try and use synesthetic layering when you're doing this. Since I keep bringing up passenger seats, let's go ahead and do that:

When Drake sat in Eazy's Buick Lesabre he immediately remembered why Eazy called it his "under-bucket." The seats and floors were littered with fast food wrappers which gave the interior a stale smell. The inside of the car was just as cold as the outside. Probably because the back passenger seat window was broken and covered with duct tape. As soon as he sat down, he was suddenly overwhelmed with the nostalgia of his younger days, before all the fast money and multiple murders. A simpler life by far...

Damn, y'all! I hit on all the senses when we stepped into Eazy's Buick. I described the smell, feeling, visuals and threw in the memories which told us a lil' bit more about them. Now, *that's* what's up!

SOUND

Life is a rainbow of sound. We are constantly surrounded by sound. We know this, so how do we put it on paper? And why should we? First of all, you should realize that most of the time when something really harsh happens, we usually walk away from that incident mostly recalling the sound we heard.

I remember a shootout I was in when I lived in Tennessee, and to this day I still remember the sharp sounds of the bullets as they whizzed passed my head. It was like a miniature airplane flying close to my head. The only way I can describe the sound is with words like sharp, airplane and fast. I'm pretty sure the bullets would've felt sharp if they hit me, and they were fast, but they didn't look like airplanes. That's what they made me think of though. That's why I added the extras, so I could describe the sound of bullets flying passed my head. That's real life, and that's what your readers want.

VISUAL

The first thing you need to remember when describing something visual is that everything you see is light. Everything we see is the product of light reflecting off any object we're looking at. Whether you're admiring the wet-like paint you just put on your whip, or the beautiful curves on the face of your lover while you're lying next to her in bed. The rays of the sun are shining on the fresh paint, and the ambient light from the television set is what's setting the tone for your lover's beauty. If you really study the way light bounces off something, or soaks into something, then you'll be able to dig deep into the vast arena of your mind to find the right words to paint the pictures you are trying to present to your readers.

As an author of urban novels you have to see your work as if it's a movie for your readers. Whenever you go to the movies you enter a dark room that will take you into another world. For that hour and a half, the actors playing in said movie are able to make you believe they are murderers, drug lords, or a damsel in distress. This is what you should be thriving to create if you want your readers to visualize and describe your book to their friends the same way they would if they had just seen a multimillion-dollar movie. And trust me, it happens. I've had multiple associates go off on tangents while describing a story they had just read. But it was cool because it just made me want to go out and find that book and read it for myself. That's what I want my books to do to my readers.

You also need to be specific on many aspects of your story. It'll help your reader visualize the scene better. Like in the scene where I described the inside of Eazy's car, just mentioning the fact that it was a Buick Lesabre triggered a picture in the mind of the reader. If the reader ever sat inside of a Lesabre his mind would've automatically associated that specific memory with that scene.

When it comes to descriptions, you're gonna have to learn your colors, too. I'm not talking about the many colors, either. I'm saying you need to know the whole set of 64 Crayola colors. I'm serious, just take a blue for instance; if your character is looking up at the sky, is it midnight blue or sky blue? When your reader is visualizing a scene it's so much fuller when you really take them there.

In a lot of urban novels, especially the ones written by women, the clothing descriptions are always on point. I've read a story where a character was really killing a lot of people, and the author made sure I knew what dude was wearing the whole time! When I write, I don't really get into the labels of clothing my characters wear, unless I'm describing a scene in which he or she is getting ready to do something where their clothing is out of the ordinary. However, sometimes it's good to describe exactly what your characters are wearing so it will cement the picture into the mind of the reader.

VOCABULARY

Your vocabulary is very important for the description process. You should constantly push yourself to use the best words when writing. Build your vocab! Don't let words slow down you're writing on your first draft, though. Just let your thoughts flow. Don't worry about your words or punctuations, just let the creative bricks fall into place. Later on, in the revision process you'll be more prepared to cherry pick which words sound better.

I always keep an old thesaurus next to my desk. That's an old friend of mine. However, that's needless to say because I'm a writer and a thesaurus and dictionary are tools of my trade. Of course, I've got a few of 'em laying around. And so should you! If you're ever at a loss for words you can pick them up and they'll get you where you need to be.

Also, give your reader a lil' credit. If someone is reading an urban novel, they have to have a little intelligence. Don't shy away from making them think. Hit them with a few similes and a couple metaphors. These two gems will actually help your reader process the information you are trying to lace them with.

A simile is a figure of speech by which two essentially unlike things are compared, the comparison being made explicit typically by the use of the introductory words like "or" and "as."

A metaphor is a figure of speech by which a thing is spoken of as being that which it only resembles.

We actually use metaphors and similes every day. Your job as a writer of urban novels is to come up with fresh ones that'll surprise and intrigue your readers. These lil' tools are what enable us to enter the minds of our readers without them knowing.

Do you have lyricism? Lyricism is when your work sounds like music to the ears of your reader. I'm not talking about rhyming your words. I'm asking if you were to read your work out loud, would it sound like the words are sliding out in perfect rhythm. This is important when you're trying to enter the mind of your reader. If your words don't flow, it impedes the whole idea you're trying to convey. If your writing is lyrical, it adds allure to the experience you are giving to your reader.

I can't emphasize enough on why you should let your writing flow during the initial writing process. Don't worry about anything, you can always change things later.

By the time you get to your final draft you'll probably

have to take some things out. If there was an area where you were rambling for three pages about what someone was wearing during a drug transaction, you can eliminate it. It's always good to include details, but sometimes you gotta ask yourself if the details you included have interrupted the flow of your story. If they do, take it out.

Sometimes you won't know which set of details are too much or too little, but once you get through your second or third draft it'll jump off the page at you. Until then, write, write, write!

CLICHÉS

There are some things you should watch for when describing things in your book. One of them is using old clichés. Here's a few examples:

"Her eyes were as cold as ice."
"He was dressed to the T."
"It smelled like death."
"He was tall, dark and handsome."
"Sharp as a tack."

Try your hardest not to take the easy way out. Your reader will get it if you hit 'em with an original. That's actually how you create a classic. All you have to do is give them the benefit of the doubt.

Oh yeah, one last note on describing people: When a person describes someone, the first thing they do is tell about eye color, hair color and height. Of course, you want to talk about all that, but your reader will feel more into your book if you tell them more. Was the character wearing a button-up that was missing a button? Did his breath smell like coffee? What about jewelry or tattoos? Stay away from dry and boring descriptions.

When someone picks up an urban novel, they know what they are about to read is fiction. What they are doing when they decide to read it is to trust you as the author. They are agreeing to trust you to take them into a world they can believe is real. It's your job to give them what they want and do it so well that they'll want more.

TEN GEMS

1. Sensual writing is when you stimulate most of your reader's senses with your writing.
2. Synesthesia is the act of using one sense to describe another.
3. It always helps to be specific on many aspects of your story, because it'll help your reader visualize the setting better.
4. Learn all 64 of the Crayola colors.
5. Keep a thesaurus and dictionary close by.
6. Sprinkle your urban novel with similes and metaphors.
7. Lyricism is when your work sound like music to the ears of your reader.
8. Avoid using clichés.
9. When describing your characters, be unique and tell your readers something about them that they'll remember.
10. Write, write, write! Worry about corrections later.

CHAPTER THIRTEEN

Setting

Does setting matter? Anyone who reads urban novels can give you the answer to that question. Of course, it matters, and I'm gonna give you more than a few reasons as to why that is. Before I get started I wanna state that a lot of readers take setting for granted. Most urban novels take place in cities and ghettos, so the story will include drugs, gangs, and violence. But that's not the only reason urban novels are set up in the inner cities. The setting of your story establishes the mood, feeling and point of view of your story. It immediately drops your reader into the middle of your story. If the facts and details regarding your setting are true your reader will trust you even more, and that's the best way to start a journey.

SETTING THE MOOD

Just like lighting candles and turning on slow jams will set the mood for romance, there are also ways to set the mood in your story. The whole point is to take your reader away from their reality and into the world you have created. Therefore, you'll have to alter their mood in order for the experience to seem real.

Imagine a scene where the character is a high maintenance female, she's at home all dressed up, ready to go out with her boyfriend. She spent most of her day getting ready for this date, but now her man is 30 minutes late. She keeps calling him, yet the phone goes straight to voicemail. What she doesn't realize is that her date is stuck in a major traffic jam across town, and he accidently left his phone on the entertainment center at his house. The couple had already been having problems; that this date was supposed to help patch things up from their last argument.

The scene I just described can set the mood for anger or jealousy. That situation is a great way to build tension and an even better opportunity to utilize the tool I spoke of earlier, which is understanding. The reader knows the details, but the characters don't. At the same time, opening the door for all kinds of options depending on the characters and what's going on in their lives.

LET'S GET COMFORTABLE...

Awhile back, I was watching a movie that started out at a beautiful family gathering. All the children and adults were having a great time on the beach. It was a nice sunny day and all the partygoers were dressed in white from head to toe. The setting was nice, bright and comfortable. Then, a crew of masked gunmen suddenly showed up and started shooting; total pandemonium broke out. The gunmen were there to massacre the whole family, and that's what they did, right down to the youngest child.

The opening scene was a total contrast to what took place seconds after I got comfortably into that movie. It really put me into the action, because I was just settling into the calmness of the family scene. The setting in that movie did that, and you as an author can create that as well. There are plenty of situations that can arouse those same type of feelings from your readers, just as long as you control your settings.

ERA

One of my all-time favorite urban novels is "A Huster's Wife." At the beginning of that story the author placed me in the late 1980's with the kind of music he had playing, the clothing that he had the characters wearing, and the styles of hair they were sporting. The story eventually worked its way into the millennium. By the end of the book I felt as if I had watched the characters grow up. It's a real cool story, and it's a perfect example on how an author can control the time period of an urban novel by its setting. When you're writing about past eras you have to pay extra attention to your details.

One minor foul-up can turn your reader against you. A mistake like having your characters text each other before the internet existed. Or putting 28" rims on a car before those sizes even existed. However, you can easily show a character is out of touch with current styles by having them wear clothing that doesn't fit that era. Like in the scene from the movie "I'm gonna get you sucka," when the pimp gets out of prison wearing bell-bottoms, after doing over a decade in prison. That character was stuck in the 70's, but he didn't know any better because of how long he had been locked down.

VIEW POINT

Don't forget that your narrator is the one who is telling the story. Therefore, you'll have to see the setting through his eyes. Maybe your narrator is the person who is fresh out of prison, and he is the one who isn't up on the latest styles. Instead of your readers watching other people's reaction to him, they'd get his take on the culture shock he was experiencing after doing over a decade in prison. Even his vocabulary and mannerisms would be affected by his time away from society.

Or, maybe your protagonist has to leave the country for

some reason. How does he view this new environment he's in? Is it hostile? How does he see the differences? If your reader agrees with your character's point of view, then this can build a connection between him and your protagonist. Your goal is to help your reader experience this journey with the character. It's also what your readers want, so give it to 'em.

PLACE

When writers talk about "place" they are speaking about any specific location, no matter how big or small. From country, state, city, neighborhood, street, house and room. Where ever the character is at, what it looks like, smells like and feels like. The whole point is to put your reader there. Take them from point "A" which is where they have opened your book, to point "B" which is a specific place in your urban novel.

You should always be aware of where your characters are and constantly let your readers know it. Some places need more describing than others. Nevertheless, regardless of how unimportant the place is, don't ever just leave your character in a square white room. Put them in a place surrounded by objects and describe it to your readers.

Don't forget that places and settings do matter in your story. It can add mystery and intrigue that your reader can figure out for himself, or share with the characters in the story. Imagine a person walking towards your protagonist on a busy street on South Beach in Miami. It's a hot summer day and the mysterious person is wearing a dark blue hoody. That might not stick out if the setting was a cool autumn evening in New York; but in the Miami setting it has drama written all over it. Does your character see this guy goading towards him? Do you tell your reader that the dark character is clutching a pistol underneath his sweater? A scene like that will have your reader at the edge of his seat, trying to send the character a message that he'll never hear...

If the settings and places don't match the action in your story, you need to go back and change it. You gotta have setting.

Most authors write about places they've been to or grew up in. That's good because it enables them to write about real details describing the cities they're writing about. If the reader has actually been to the place they're reading about, and they see that the facts are true, that adds credence to everything else that writer created.

If you decide to write about a place, you have never been to it's extremely important that you do your homework, so that you can obtain as much accurate information as you can. If you can't get to the internet from where you're at then go find a map out of an Almanac or something. If you try to make up some facts and you get them wrong, you run the risk of losing your reader.

An easy out for this part is making up a fictional location. Instead of writing about San Juan, Puerto Rico, create your own Island like St. Holizon or Puerto Velde. But if you choose to make up a fictional island then your whole story should take place in or throughout fictional locations, otherwise you risk confusing your reader when you take them from real to fake.

Also, be selective in the places you describe. Just because you just learned that setting matters it doesn't mean that you should go cray-cray on places and spend the same amount of time on each setting. I mentioned it earlier and I'll say it again: You will describe some places in more detail than others. However, you'll need to ask yourself as the author; which place needs more description?

It helps to envision your scene from the beginning. When I covered dialogue, I told you that dialogue should be reserved for important scenes, and that's true. But in order for you to make a major scene in your urban novel you'll have to make the setting as realistic as possible. Put your reader there, right next to the conversation. And the only way to accomplish this is by describing the setting.

RESEARCHING YOUR LOCATIONS

You can always set your story in your city and neighborhood, but it adds depth to any plot when the characters leave or get taken out of their comfort zone. It adds action to a plot when the protagonist travels. So don't get stuck in a box, spread your wings and travel. The catch is that you need to be factual. Learn everything you can about the locations you decide to add in your story. Don't go overboard when it comes to laying down your newfound knowledge on paper, though. You don't want to make yourself sound like an Almanac, or a tourist. Yet, you do want to put your readers there.

The setting to your story can also tell the reader a lot about your characters. If your protagonist grew up in Chattanooga, Tennessee, it'd be a fact that this character would have a totally different swagger than a facts-paced youngster who came up in Queens, New York. The slowed down country setting where the projects in Tennessee are placed would definitely create a different person than the high-rise housing projects, with multiple races of people, which populate a major metropolitan city like Queens. Always keep this in mind while you're working on the setting for your urban novel.

TEN GEMS

1. The setting of your story establishes the mood, feeling, and point of view of your urban novel.

2. When writing about past eras you have to watch your details, because one foul-up can turn the reader against you.

3. You'll have to show your reader the setting through the eyes of your narrator.

4. You should constantly be aware of where your characters are and let your readers know it.

5. If the setting or places in your urban novel doesn't affect the action in your story, then go back and tweak your manuscript.

6. If you decide to write about a place where you have never been to it's extremely important that you do your homework so that you can obtain as much accurate information as you can.

7. An easy way out from researching a place is to create a fictional place.

8. Be selective when choosing which places to describe.

9. Envision each scene from the beginning.

10. The setting to your story can tell your reader a lot about your characters, so keep this in mind when working on setting.

CHAPTER FOURTEEN

Pace

Before we get too deep into this chapter, I need to make sure everyone is on board with the actual meaning of the word "pace." The pace of a story is the speed at which characters are introduced and events play out. If you need it explained mathematically:

You divide the amount of major situations by the page count. The higher the ratio means the faster the pace.

Writing fast paced urban novels is not for everyone. However, there is a common knowledge among writers and their readers that says, if you don't snatch your reader's attention within the first fifty pages, chances are, they're gonna put that book down. Especially in this age of low attention spans, readers need to be drawn into a story real quick or it just won't work. Why else do you think I keep telling you to start your urban novel in the middle of some action?

I've mentioned the fact that you should start your story in the middle of some action. But I haven't gone on to explain that the tension you create in the first fifty pages of your urban novel needs to drive your readers all the way through your story until they reach the climax. The drama you start with should have some kind of connection to the plot of the story. Don't start you story with a shoot-out if that shoot-out isn't connected with the main plot of your book. If you start your story with an attention-grabbing scene that has nothing to do with the plot of your novel, it'll create a mistrust between you and your reader.

By the end of the first fifty pages your protagonist should be facing major issues. Your urban novel doesn't really start until the main character is experiencing some kind of turmoil; which has to be caused by the main objective of the story, which is the goal. Basically, your main character has to be in some deep shit by the end of the first fifty pages.

You might be wondering how you're gonna manage to get your reader involved in your urban novel so early without knowing the background of your story. If this is an issue for you then sit back and think about it. Ask yourself what it is that your reader has to know before you catapult into action. Most of the time you won't have to give them as much as you think.

If you want to give your beginning a twist, start out with a prologue. A prologue is where you start with a scene that happens in the middle of your story. For instance, if you have a plot where you start off the story with two best friends who hustle together, but at some point one of them kills the other, a good idea for a prologue is a scene where one is burying the other.

If you really want to add some tension, don't tell your reader which character is doing the digging. As the story plays out, your reader will be looking forward to the sinister scene that reveals the Judas. That's the first step in creating a page turner.

You have a lot to accomplish in those first fifty pages, but if done correctly your reader will be hooked. Not only must you start your urban novel in the middle of the action, you also have to introduce the protagonist, and lay down the rules of your story. What I mean by "laying down the rules" is that during those first 50 pages you'll be giving your reader a glimpse at how your urban novel will be written, whose p.o.v. the story will be narrated by, and the techniques you'll be using to give them this world.

Once your reader knows how the story will be told they can sit back and enjoy the ride. If you are gonna tell your story through multiple p.o.v.'s you should introduce at least two characters within the first 50 pages. If you don't, you run the risk of confusing your reader. And that's not a good way to start off the relationship you are trying to build with the reader.

Whoever picks up your urban novel and decides to start reading is trusting you to take them on a safe ride through the world you have created. They are expecting plots, twists, characters, and an escape from real life. So, give them what they want, and give it to them within the first fifty pages so they'll stay motivated to keep turning pages.

So far, we've covered the first 50 pages. Now, let's get back to pacing or manipulating the time in your story. You're going to need this knowledge since this is how you will either compress or expand scenes in your urban novel.

When time passes for your characters, it is you who controls it. From the birth of your character to his death, it's all on you. Of course, you're not gonna show every second of your plot. You are only going to give your readers what they need to know. Therefore, it's up to you to either slow down or speed up certain sections of the plot. It's up to you to choose which scenes are important to your readers. With this in mind; you should get your worth out of the ones you do choose.

One of the main ways to accomplish pacing is being able to alternate your story from scene to summary. Remember, a scene is when something important is happening, and summary is when you give the scene to the reader without the actual details of it playing out in real time.

Since we're working on urban novels you have more space to work with than if you were writing a short story. However, you're still gonna have to pay attention to how much space you have to work with. You want to give your reader enough to enjoy the full experience.

FLASHBACKS

Another trick to this trade is called flashbacks. Flashbacks help the most when you need to explain something that took place prior to where you're at in your story. You might want to give your reader a little piece of the past. You can do this by drifting back to another time in the life of one of your characters. This will also enable your readers to empathize with your characters more deeply.

It's not a good idea to rely on flashbacks too much, though. If you find yourself using flashbacks too often it usually means you started your story at the wrong point in time. This can confuse your reader, giving them the feeling that your story is disorganized. How many times do you want to stop for gas when you're painting the town?

SLOW OR FAST?

Pace, like everything else in writing doesn't come without its trade-offs. If you're writing a slow-paced novel, you obviously aren't giving your reader much action. So, you should at least give them something else. A slow-paced urban novel is ideal for character development. If you're trying to create a story where your readers can form a deep interest in your characters then a slow-paced story will give you the room and space to develop that relationship.

Conflict drives urban novels. No one wants to read a story where it all goes smoothly. A faster paced story gives you more opportunities to get your character into trouble. Conflict maintains as well as creates tension. Tension is what keeps your readers at the edge of their seats while they turn the pages. Your reader's sole purpose will be to find out how your characters will get themselves out of trouble. Specifically, the trouble you've created for them.

Here's how you can slow a scene down. I took this

excerpt directly out of my urban novel titled *Devils & Demons*. And as a side note; anyone who has ever experienced any kind of gunplay can relate to this because for some reason time can really slow down when you're in the midst of life-or-death violence.

...Before she could even finish her statement, a deep banging sound came from the door to the room. It sounded like someone was trying to kick it open. Suddenly, the door snapped off its hinges and came crashing onto the floor. Everyone was caught off guard, giving Talton the edge he needed. It took a second for Yada, the sole person in the room with a gun, to assess the threat and reach for his weapon. Still, he was too slow.

As if his brother's OP medallion was a hone-in device, Talton zeroed in on it immediately. Ignoring everyone else in the room, he stepped in with his cannon in shooting position and quickly let off four deafening rounds, all of them aimed straight into his target's face. Upon impact, the bullets exploded, causing blood and brain matter to be grossly discarded in all directions, but mostly against the sliding glass door where Yada's lifeless body had fallen against.

In Talton's mind everything was moving in slow motion. Alize ran towards another female, whom he didn't recognize, and they both sprinted towards the door. That's when he saw the dread sitting on the couch. This had to be the "Nirobi" character that the other one had called after killing Ant. Therefore, in Talton's eyes, he was an accomplice.

Talton slowly lifted his Desert Eagle, wanting to savor the moment. When Nirobi realized that was happening, he dived off the couch, but it was too late. Boom! Boom! Boom! Fire shot out the tip of the gun every time Talton pulled his finger. Nirobi's torso flipped sideways as the bullets destroyed his upper chest cavity.

That's when Gangsta heard Alize trying to get his attention, but his mind didn't register what she was saying. He needed Ant's necklace; it was a piece of his brother, and he had to have it. With only one thing on his mind, Talton dropped his gun and walked towards his first victim.

The headless body lay slumped against the glass door, still spitting blood from its main artery. The man's heart must have missed the memo. It was over; there was no way he was coming back from that. Talton walked over to the dead body, reached down, and snatched Anthony's bloody necklace from the marauder's neck. He then put it on, letting it rest next to its twin.

That's when the world around Talton began to speed up. Now he could hear and understand what Alize was trying to tell him. From the doorway, she was yelling, "Hurry up! Come on, Talton!" Then in the background, he heard a man's voice, "Call the police!" That woke Talton all the way up. Alize ran towards her car. Talton followed, but he stopped just short of the door....

Here's a few tricks that'll help you speed up the pace in your urban novel:

1.   Start your urban novel in the middle of some drama, not before it.

2.   Keep your descriptions to a minimum. Yeah, paint a picture, but let their imagination do the rest.

3.   Remix the scenes. If you have two scenes that take place one after the other, put them together. If your protagonist does a drug deal and later on finds out the dope was fake, remix those two scenes to make him find out the deal was a sham during the transaction.

4.   Use conversation. That's what we have dialogue for, to make a scene. Much of a story can be told through dialogue. Look at Shakespeare; that dude got famous from telling stories through spoken dialogue.

5.   Keep historical date to a minimum. The pace tends to slow down during flashbacks and memories. Let your reader learn about your characters from what they are doing

now.

6.   Shorten your chapters. Read a James Patterson novel. This'll show you how a professional manipulates short chapters while keeping tensions high at the same time.

7.   Another way of increasing the pace of your story is by eliminating every unnecessary word. There are times you may want to slow down a scene and describe a majestic background. That's cool, but if you really want to quicken the pace, take out all the poetry.

Faster isn't always better. Every author has his or her own individual style of writing. I'm not about to sit here and tell anyone that one way is better than the other. Yet, I will say this though: In this genre, the faster the pace, the better.

TEN GEMS

1.   The pace of a story is the speed at which characters are introduced and events play out.

2.   If you don't catch your reader's attention within the first 50 pages, chances are, they'll put your book down.

3.   The drama you start your story with should have some connection to the main plot.

4.   If you want to give your beginning a twist, start off with a prologue.

5.   One of the main ways to accomplish pacing is being able to alternate from scene to summary.

6.   If you find yourself using flashbacks too much, that usually means you started your story at the wrong point in time.

7.   A slow-paced story is ideal for character development.

8.   A fast-paced story gives you more opportunity to get your characters in trouble.

9.   Conflict creates and maintains tension.

10. Tension is what is going to keep your readers at the edge of their seats.

CHAPTER FIFTEEN

Voice

It's time to talk about the voice of your story. I call it "voice" because it's the sound that your readers are going to be hearing in their heads as they experience the trip through your story. It'll also be the same sound they hear in their heads after they finish reading your urban novel. This "sound" is the voice of the narrator.

This sound is a big part of why I like to write so much. How can someone create a sound when all he has is ink and paper? And I'm not talking about musical notes, either. It's the creation of a vibe that you introduce to your readers that will create a voice in their minds without ever having to pick up a phone and speaking to you. That's what I call art!

What I'm gonna do now is discuss a few different kinds of voices with you. This will give you an idea of the various tricks of the trade you can use while creating your work.

One of the first rules to choosing a voice for your urban novel is that your voice will have to be connected to the point of view that you'll be telling your story from. Since the p.o.v. is the p.o.v. of whoever is telling the story to your reader, it's his voice your reader will hear. This means the voice is going to need to match the personality of the character who is telling the story.

A first-person narrator is, of course, going to be close to that action because he's in the story. But this won't be the case with a second- or third-person narrative. All these factors will dictate the emotional closeness of the voice to the story.

If you want to get a better sense of what I'm saying, look at it as if it's a football game. After the game a reporter will ask one of the players his take on what happened. The player was playing, so you'll get that perspective. Now think of how the coach of the winning team would describe it. He's the one who called the shots, but he never got dirty. Finally, think about how the sportscaster would describe that same game.

He was there, yet he never got dirty, nor did he call any of the plays. All of the voices I just described will all tell the same story, but from three different perspectives.

CONVERSATIONAL VOICE

A lot of writers choose a conversational voice because it's the most casual form of them all. I'd basically describe that as the voice I'm using to write this book you're reading right now.

A conversational voice is mostly used in first person p.o.v. and the speech patterns include ebony. It's just like talking to one of your friends. The best part of this voice is that you can bring your protagonist to life and have him meet the reader. This will give your reader a chance to look at his personality as the story unfolds. The problem with this voice is that sometimes he won't shut-up, and there are times when that can take away from the story and action at hand.

INFORMAL VOICE

An informal voice is one step away from the conversational voice. You'll still be telling the story in a conversational tone, but it won't be as casual. You won't be holding a conversation with the reader. This voice will still utilize slang and talk in everyday language, but he won't have as much personality as the conversational voice.

The best part of using this voice is that you get the best of both worlds. You'll have the opportunity to talk to your readers which will actually help them forget that the writer's doing the talking. And you won't take away from the story or the characters in it. A lot of urban novel writers choose this voice since it's the easiest to stick with.

FORMAL VOICE

Now we're gonna enter a whole other realm of narrating. When you decide to use a formal voice it's time to get a little more serious. First of all, your formal voice isn't gonna use ebonix, and he definitely won't be holding a conversation with the reader. This voice will be telling the story with a certain detachment from the characters.

This is the better choice when you're telling a longer story with a slower pace. If your urban novel is going to have a lot of characters, and include a substantial amount of travelling, this would be the best choice because it'll give your story a serious vibe.

It's best to choose an informal voice when you're telling the story in third person. It'll give your urban novel a more sophisticated feel. However, you can also use it in first person p.o.v. if your character has a sophisticated swagger.

I'm the first person to tell everyone I know to try and think outside the box every chance you get. It's really okay to steer off the road if you feel like it. First and foremost, you must "do you." If there's a particular voice you find yourself using to guide the reader through your urban novel, then use it. There are times in life when you have to be unique. If you feel like this is one of those times then make it happen, captain!

I once read a book narrated by the Grim Reaper. A third person, informal voice was used but the character was the Grim Reaper. He told me how he felt about picking up the souls of dead people. And that worked for me. He was actually one of the most memorable characters in the story even though he didn't play a part in the plot. I chew on that for a minute.

STYLE

In this chapter there have been more than enough sentences where I could've changed the word "voice" to "style," but I didn't. The reason for this is the "style" and "voice" mean two different things. STYLE is how you put all your words together, and how you write. VOICE is the sound that comes from the way you decide to put the words together.

Voice is the personality that comes from that. Have you ever heard two people argue, yet they were actually defending the same point? They were both arguing the same point, but their delivery was different, so they both thought they were disagreeing. It probably happened because both parties were using different words. If you wanted to you can write a paragraph using three syllable words which will make that paragraph sound more formal than another that is saying the same thing, but using smaller words.

In the end, choosing the right words to narrate your urban novel is up to you. If you're telling a story where the narrator is conversational, then chances are he won't be using 3- and 4-syllable words. Sometimes you'll make mistakes, the wrong word will sneak in, and it'll be up to you to find and revise your mistakes.

SYNTAX

Words aren't the only thing that'll dictate your style. It's also how you put them together to create your sentences. Some writers use long sentences, others tend to write with shorter sentences. Neither one is better than the other, but one thing is for certain, and that is that you will bore your reader if you choose to work with just one or the other. When you're writing, it's smart to switch up the lengths of your sentences or else your reader will get comfortable and they'll get lazy. You should learn to manipulate your sentences to create a certain rhythm.

PARAGRAPHS

We've covered words and sentences; now, let's talk about paragraphs. The length of your paragraphs will also affect the voice of your work. The same rules on sentence syntax should apply to paragraphs as well. You should keep switching up the length so that your work won't become boring or predictable.

A long paragraph can push a thought that is windy and serious. A short one can seem short and chatty. You can also write one sentence paragraphs. It's all on you and how you decide to manipulate the time and space in your story. The length of your paragraph can also show the energy that your voice emits. Is it a voice that tends to spend time describing things in detail, or is short, blunt and straight to the point?

A break in a paragraph can also show a change from narration to dialogue. If there is something going on during a conversation, that break in the paragraph will attract your reader to a whole different subject in the same scene. It can even change scenes all together.

Regardless of style or voice, a major note you should keep in mind on this subject is to stay consistent. Just like the first 50 pages of your urban novel will give your story's outline to your reader, it'll also give them your style. If your narrator is windy, talkative, and into describing things in detail, then you should keep 'em that way throughout the whole story.

Your two main objectives should be to stay in p.o.v., and be consistent with the voice.

Once you break away from this, you're breaking a "gentleman's agreement" with your reader. This can destroy the trust you've built as well as ruin the vibe you spent time cultivating. It can also confuse your readers, causing 'em to put your book down.

I know I seem to be putting a lot for emphasis on finding your voice, but seriously, don't worry about it. Don't let this slow down your writing; just write! Just like characters tend to become real after time, so will your voice. Be real with your readers and the rest will fall into place.

We haven't gotten too deep into revision yet, but we will. And when we do, I'll explain how your story will grow once you get to your second and third drafts. The reason I'm bringing this up now is that I want you to know that you will get another chance to roll the dice. Once you write your story, you'll know your characters better than you did when you started. This will definitely assist you in finding your voice, so be patient.

Try this: Every chance you get, stop and read every major scene in your urban novel. Read it to yourself out loud and ask yourself how it sounds. Do you feel the rhythm? Does the voice sound real? Is this what you had in mind when you were writing it? Does it sound natural or forced? If any of the sections don't feel right, change them! Fix it. Alter it.

TEN GEMS

1. The voice is what your readers will hear in their heads while they read your urban novel.

2. The voice is going to have to match the character of the narrator.

3. A conversational voice is usually used in first person p.o.v.'s.

4. Informal voice is one step away from conversational voice.

5. A formal voice will tell the story with a certain detachment from the characters.

6. Style is how you put your words together.

7. When you're writing it's smart to switch up the lengths of your sentences, or else your reader will get lazy.

8. The same rule of sentence syntax should apply to paragraphs as well.

9. Regardless of style or voice, a major note you should keep in mind on this subject is to stay consistent.

10. Your two main objectives should be to stay in p.o.v. and be consistent with the voice.

CHAPTER SIXTEEN

Theme

This aspect of craft always makes me think of my teenage years. When I was around 15 years old, I used to stay going in and out of juvenile hall. Twice a week my mom would be there to visit me. During that time Moms still had a lil' thug left over from her younger days, so she would try her hardest to lace me with as much game as she could.

During one specific visit she came in and immediately started telling me about this movie she had just seen called "Carlito's Way." She kept telling me that I had to watch this movie. She was so adamant that it was like she was gonna make me sit down and watch this flick.

The plot of the movie revolved around an ex-drug dealer trying to stack some money so he could leave the country and start a new life with his pregnant girlfriend. The problem was that all the obstacles that he came in contact with came from his friends. All throughout the movie his best friends are the cause of one problem after another. In the end, his closest comrade is the person who was ultimately responsible for his death.

This movie became a classic, like most Al Pacino flix, but the reason my mother wanted me to watch it so bad wasn't because of the plot or the actors playing the parts. It was because of the theme. "Don't trust anyone; watch your friends because they'll be the first ones to cross you." Theme is the underlying message in any story you read or write or watch play out on a movie screen.

If your goal is to write an urban novel that will imbed itself in the minds of all your readers then you better have a theme. You don't have to rack your brain looking for a theme in the first draft of your book, but at one point or another you're gonna have to come up with one. If you don't have a theme your readers will probably assume one on their own anyway. However, chances are, your urban novel won't flow as smoothly as it would if you had one.

You gotta watch yourself, though. Even though you need to know what your theme is, you should also make sure you don't overdo it. If you get too caught up in trying to explain your theme, your story will get boring. It'll seem like you're trying to preach, and that's not what your readers came for. The theme should really creep into their conscious, not be stuffed down their throats. Don't worry about your readers catching the theme because that's where they'll surprise you. Give 'em the benefit of the doubt. If you do what you're supposed to, they'll get it.

If you want to dodge the pitfalls of overdoing your theme, don't start your urban novel trying to explain your motive. Start your story with that fifty page dash that I wrote about earlier. If you begin your book with theme in mind, nine times out of ten, you'll end up preaching and that's not cool. Just tell your story. In time your theme will begin to show itself.

A lot of times your theme won't materialize until you finish writing the first draft.

Even if you started writing your book with a specific idea in mind, it might change after you sit down and read your first draft. And that's closure. That's how it's supposed to happen. The best themes emerge from a story in progress.

Here a few questions you should ask yourself if you want to figure out a theme for your urban novel:

1. Does your character make moves that represent a universal truth?

2. Does your main character, beating his arch-enemy, represent David beating Goliath?

3. Is your theme about downfalls of addiction?

4. Does your protagonist choose a beautiful woman over a mediocre one or an ugly one – just to come out with his heart broken?

5. Is your urban novel about death?

6. What made you start writing your story in the first place?

After you answer these questions, something should hop off the page at you. Chances are the theme was there the whole time. Sometimes you'll find something about yourself that you didn't know before. Just answer the questions and you'll see what I'm talking about.

What you really need to do is look at your first draft. Find anything that is recurring in your story, and look for any repeating words or images. Most of the time your theme is buried in there somewhere.

When you finally find the theme, you should write it in bold letters on a piece of paper and tape it over your work area. This way you can be reminded of your theme while you work.

Your theme is gonna touch everything in your story once you start revising. If your story is about distrust then little things in your story will start to take on a new meaning. A scene where your protagonist pauses to make eye contact with another character before answering a question can now be a sign of distrust. By knowing your theme and working with it your story will automatically grow and become deeper.

In the next chapter I'll be discussing the revision process. You'll find out that after you finish your first draft there will be a lot of taking out and adding things. Being in tune with your theme will help you decide whether to keep a scene, or delete it from your story. It's all part of the writing process. Once you figure out your theme, and you go back to revise your story, you'll realize that it adds depth.

The repetition of thematic events will start to add up, and that's what you ultimately want. Thematic repetition is good. This is how you'll show your readers what your story is all about.

These are all key elements in being able to reach inside the minds of your readers. If you are serious about creating a classic you need to study these elements.

TEN GEMS

1. If you want to imbed your urban novel into the mind of your reader you'll have to have a theme.

2. Don't worry about finding the theme in your first draft.

3. Your urban novel won't flow smoothly if you don't have a theme.

4. Don't get caught up trying to explain your theme.

5. The theme should creep into your reader's conscious, not be stuffed down their throats.

6. Never start your story trying to explain your theme.

7. A theme will usually emerge from work in progress.

8. A good way to find your theme is to look for recurring words or images.

9. Your theme should touch everything in your story.

10. Thematic repetition is good.

CHAPTER SEVENTEEN

Revision

Revision is one of the most important aspects of writing. When I wrote my first manuscript, I hated the idea of revising it. Since I had no training in writing whatsoever, I thought my first draft, with all the work I had put into it, was enough. The result was garbage, and that first book made it into a trash can.

The more I studied this craft, the more I started to see that revising is actually part of the writing process. Since I realized this, I actually started enjoying it. Every time I revise a chapter, I get the satisfying feeling that I just got that much closer to finishing my project. It also gives me the opportunity to add meat to an already thick sandwich, or sometimes, take out some of the lettuce so I could taste more meat. Either way, revising always makes the outcome better.

It's also like buying an old-school whip that needs some work. The first things you want to work on are the engine and transmission. After that, you know you have a dependable vehicle. Now you need to get the interior done, and then some music. When that's finished, the car rides nice, feels nice, and sounds like you've got a gorilla in the trunk. The last thing you want to do when flippin' an old school is the body work and paint. The day you pull it out the shop you'll feel like you own the streets. I know because I've done it on several occasions. And revising my urban novels gives me that same feeling.

Revising is the process of shining up your work. Your first draft is usually trash.

I hate to call anyone's work trash, and I know some of you will take that last statement rather harsh, but that's only because you've fallen in love with your work, or better yet, your first draft. You're never supposed to do that. It's okay if your first draft isn't platinum, it's not supposed to be.

Whenever you start writing a story, you shouldn't worry about anything else other than getting your thoughts on paper. Forget punctuation, handwriting, or even order. Just write. Try and unleash all of your ideas on paper without trippin' off anything else. Your first draft is like you're diggin' for that giant diamond. You can worry about cut, clarity, and color later. Right now, you're diggin' through that mine in your head.

FOUR STEPS TO REVISION

The whole purpose of revising is to polish your urban novel into its ultimate form. What I'm gonna do is break down the revision process into four elements. If done correctly, you will be able to watch your work metamorphism into something worth letting loose into the world for the masses to enjoy. This four-step plan is meant to be done one method at a time. This will give you four to five revisions, and that's more than enough revising to get the job done. It's best to do one chapter at a time. What I'm saying is, get one chapter down on paper then revise that chapter. Instead of writing your whole book then going back to revise the whole thing.

The reason I recommend that you only do one chapter at a time is because during the revision process you'll be doing a lot of rethinking on characters and plot, so you'll be choppin' and screwing your work. If you wait until you've finished your whole urban novel you might get stuck wanting to change the whole story around.

STEP 1: STRUCTURE

- Your goal is to create a clear and concise plot structure.
- You're looking for slow-moving scenes and boring dialogues.
- The remedy is to make sure your scenes are in order and that your chapter isn't dull or anticlimactic.
- Each chapter is like a mini story within a story. The end of a chapter marks a section in your urban novel where your reader can take a break from reading. So every chapter should have a beginning, a middle, and end. The beginning is when you introduce the conflict in which your chapter will revolve around. The middle of the chapter is when that problem gets complicated, and the end is when that complication gets solved.

A slow-paced dialogue is when characters are talking about nothing. Dialogues should be used to move plot along, and build characterization. The most interesting conversations in a story are those built around drama. A tension filled dialogue builds a tension filled scene, which makes your urban novel more interesting. This is what you're trying to create in this step of the revision process.

STEP 2: TEXTURE

- Your goal is to build the descriptive parts of your story like characters, setting and action.
- You're looking for sections that have either too much or too little description.
- The remedy is painting a picture that will put your reader in the car with your characters.

Many writers add way too many details to their descriptions. That isn't always necessary. Sometimes it comes in the form of telling your readers too much about a person or a place. This can slow your story down as well as bore some of your readers. I've met a few individuals who are avid fans of urban novels, but these same people wouldn't give a Stephen King novel the time of day. The reason is that Stephen King's books move way too slow. He adds too many details. Maybe it's because he gets paid by the word, and this isn't what the average fan of urban novels is looking for.

Then again, too little description can be just as annoying. Even though you might tell your reader a character is in a car, they might not get the full sense of that scene unless you a paint a picture of that car for your reader to experience.

What you need to do is dig through your work and figure out what to keep, take out, or add. You don't want to give your readers a whole bunch of information that they don't need to know, but you do want to give them just enough to put them next to your characters.

STEP 3: DIALOGUE

- Your goal is to build the personalities of your characters.
- You're looking for tag lines such as she said/ he said in the wrong places, at the wrong times.
- Your remedy is to eliminate some of these tag lines. Most of the time your reader knows whose speaking.

Dialogue isn't always all about what your characters say as much as it is about what they mean. If you sit around and listen to everyday dialogue, you'll see that it isn't always logical. Real life conversations never sound recorded, and they definitely don't sound like a newsreel. Sounding like a newsreel is what you're trying to stay away from.

Pay attention to scene summary ratio. A good writer can squeeze all these in together to create a fast-paced story that manages to keep all his readers involved. You can move a story along with scene and summary, but dialogue is what will show them who your characters really are. You can tell a lot about people by the way they talk.

STEP 4: EDITING

- Your goal is to tighten up the pace of your story, and nail everything together.
- You're looking for slow and repetitive scenes.
- The remedy is to dispose of them!

In the beginning of this chapter, I mentioned something about some of you fallin' in love with your first draft. Editing is the step that you will dislike the most. In your editing phase you're gonna be taking out all of the unnecessary parts of your urban novel. You'll be taking out sentences and words that repeat things your readers already know. You'll have to give the reader some credit. Most of the time he'll get what you're trying to tell 'em the first time around.

This is the step where you'll be making sure scenes transition smoothly into one another, and your spelling and punctuation is corrected. You handle all of this and you'll be ready for the business end of this process, which we'll be discussing in the upcoming chapters.

TEN GEMS

1. Revision is one of the most important elements of the writing process.
2. Revising is the process of shining up your work.
3. Whenever you begin writing a story, you shouldn't worry about anything else other than getting your thoughts on paper.
4. When revising, it's best work on one chapter at a time.
5. Every chapter should have a beginning, middle and

end.

6. Dialogue should be used to move plot along, and build characterization.

7. It isn't always necessary to add a lot of details.

8. You can move a story along with scene and summary, but dialogue is what will show them who your characters really are.

9. Never fall in love with your first draft.

10. Revision will turn your urban novel from a lump of coal into a priceless gem.

CHAPTER EIGHTEEN

Check List

You just finished the craft section of this book; it's almost time for you to get down and dirty about your business. But first we need to review a few things to make sure you understand everything I've covered so far. Then I'll hand over the blueprint for the business end of this cipher. As long as you pay attention and take heed to my wisdom it should be all good for those of you who are willing to put your all into it.

CHARACTERS

- Do your characters have desire?
- Do your characters have contradictory traits that make them complex?
- Are your characters distinctive enough not to be stereotypes?
- Are your characters consistent despite their contrasting traits?
Do your characters have the ability to change?
- Do you know your characters well enough?
- Are you "showing" your characters instead of "telling" them?
- Are you utilizing all four methods of showing? Action, speech, appearance and thought?

- Do your characters have the right names?

PLOT

- Does your story have a major dramatic question?
- Do you have a protagonist with a strong goal and plenty of obstacles?
- Does your protagonist have both external and internal obstacles?
- Does your urban novel have a beginning, middle and end?
- Does your main conflict escalate into the middle?
- Are the events in the middle linked by cause and effect?
- Do you have the three C's at the end? Crisis, climax and consequence?
- Is your ending realistic, satisfying, and not too long?

POINT OF VIEW

- Which p.o.v. does your story sound better coming from? First person, second person, or third person?
- If you're using a second- or third-person narrator, how close emotionally is the narrator to the characters and the story?
- Is there some reason why your urban novel might work better with the all-knowing p.o.v.?
- Are you keeping your p.o.v. consistent?

DESCRIPTION

- Are you utilizing all five senses during the descriptions?
- Are your descriptions specific enough?
- Does your work sound lyrical?

- Are your descriptions overdone?

Do your descriptions reflect the consciousness of your chosen p.o.v.?

DIALOGUE

- Are you using dialogue and scene for the more important parts of your story?
- Does your dialogue sound real?
- Do the tag lines attract too much attention to themselves?
- Are you utilizing body language to enhance your dialogue?
- Do your characters sound different than one another?

SETTING

- Have you grounded your story in a specific time and place?
- Does the place and time of your urban novel affect the action?
- Are there opportunities to let the setting enhance the atmosphere or mood?
- Do your characters act in a way that reflects their comfort or discomfort with their setting?
- Are you describing your setting so much that it slows down the action?
- Have you chosen the right places to expand, or compress time?

VOICE

- Have you picked a voice that works in harmony with the personality of your narrator, and the narrator's distance to the story?

- Does your voice stay consistent throughout the story?

THEME

- Have you identified a theme for your story?
- Does your theme engulf your story with a light enough touch?
- Do all of the elements of your story support the theme?

REVISION

- Have you fallen out of love with your story enough to start the revision process?
- Have you considered envisioning your story?
- Have you looked through a magnifying glass at all the big things in your story?
- Have you looked through a microscope at all the little things in your story?
- Have you chopped and screwed as much as you can in our urban novel?

CHAPTER NINETEEN

Business: Traditional Route

Now it's the time we get to the money. Throughout this project I've been referring to all of your work in progress as art and that's because that is what it is. Writing a book is creating art, but at the same time, you are producing a product. Your urban novel is a product that you have produced in hopes of turning a profit. At this point in the game you must come to this realization, and roll with it.

If you ever want to get your work published you have to accomplish one thing: You must finish your project. We just finished more than enough chapters on craft. If you mix that in with determination, discipline, and dedication, you have what it takes to put your stories on paper. So, do it! You'll never get a book published if all you have is ideas, or if you only have a few chapters written. It's just not gonna happen, especially for a beginner. Your first step in the business of writing urban novels is to finish your work!

To sell your work you're gonna need to send a copy of your manuscript to either an agent or an editor. If you don't want your product to just get thrown in a box along with the 100's of other manuscripts that regularly get discarded, you'll have to make your work look professional. You can't send some grimy looking papers with all kinds of creases and stains on 'em. That's not professional, and it definitely won't help sell your book. No one will take your work seriously if you don't even take yourself seriously.

The following list is the standard format for submitting your urban novel to an editor:

- use black in on white, 8.5 by 11-inch paper
- choose a 12-point font, preferably new roman, or courier
- double space
- indent paragraphs
- place at least 1 inch margin all the way around
- number pages in the upper right-hand corner
- spell check and proof read your work before you send it
- include a title page with the title, word count, your name, address, and any other contact information you may have
- Keep the page loose leaf

When your urban novel is typed up clean and legible it'll be ready to be sent out. You'll need to include a cover letter, but we'll get to that in a minute. First, you should put your book in a large manila envelope, along with a self-addressed stamped envelope, and a little note letting the publisher know that you would appreciate a reply after they read your manuscript. If you want your manuscript back, you'll want to include another large envelope with postage. If you don't send a SASE you're basically saying you don't want a reply.

Now don't start getting all paranoid about your work getting stolen. Reputable publishers aren't likely to steal your ideas. Why? Because they don't wanna run the risk of getting sued when it'd be a lot easier to just buy your urban novel for the low-low. Their hustle is to buy and sell your book, not steal and sell your work. Plus, federal law states that your urban novel is copyrighted the minute you put it on paper. If you point this out in your query, you'll make yourself look bootsy, so please don't do it to yourself. They know what's up.

QUERY LETTER

You finished your book, it's typed up clean, and you're ready to send it out. The next step is writing a query letter. The query letter is a short letter giving the publisher certain necessary information about your book that should pique your publisher's attention and entice them to read your manuscript. This is an outline for a query letter:

- An opening line or two introducing your urban novel, as well as explaining why you contacted this specific publisher. Maybe they are at the top of their game when it comes to publishing this genre.
- A quick pitch of your product. Showcase characters and situations. Basically, like a book jacket. Intrigue, don't explain. You won't need to write more than a paragraph on this one.
- Information about yourself. Don't try too hard, just give them a sense of who you are. Include anything that has to do with writing, like credits, personal or professional expertise relating to the subject matter, etc. If you don't have any experience, don't trip, a lot of writers don't.
- To end it, state that you've included a self-addressed envelope and that you look forward to a response.

The beginning of this letter should include the publisher, agents, or editor's full name. Not dear, sir, or ma'am. This is important, because it will also demonstrate your writing style. Make it sound good and they'll want to read your work.

Most initial screenings are done by assistants who are trained to look for certain things. If your query letter is weak, and not well written, it won't make it past the assistant. So, make it look good and you might make it into the hands of an interested editor.

If you're a true fan of urban novels then you've probably noticed that the majority of them are published by certain companies. These specific companies specialize in this genre, so these are the publishers you should be contacting when you are trying to get your book published.

Going to a book store is also a good place to start. When you go into a book store you'll immediately see what the covers of other urban novels look like, and if you take a closer look you'll find out who publishes them. These are the companies you need to contact. A lot of people like to go big and contact the larger companies. That's cool. Bigger isn't always better (just ask any of my baby mammas). Most of the larger companies only deal with established writers, and this might not benefit your specific situation. So don't limit yourself with just contacting the well-known companies.

MONEY

If you're going through a publishing house, you might as well learn as much as you can about the game. First, you'll have to finish your manuscript, which we've already covered. Then the manuscript is gonna have to get cleaned up and ready for publication. That's our end as writers, but the game gets deeper once it leaves our hands. The publisher has to handle the production, marketing, sale and distribution of your book. It's important that you learn as much as you can about this process, so that you can be of assistance as well as make sure no one gets over on you.

Before we go on, I want to discuss a subject that we haven't really covered yet, and that's the money subject. No matter your reason for writing urban novels, the bottom line always goes back to the money. Things are hard in here, so you gotta get it any which way you can. When I first started writing I told myself that I wasn't doing it for the money. Nevertheless, the more I wrote, the more I started thinking about getting paid for the long hours I put in on my projects. Wouldn't it be nice getting paid for doing something you like to do? And, at the same time get a lil' famous in the process?

So, book advances average from five thousand to twenty-five thousand, the higher end going to established writers who already have a history of creating good work and selling millions of copies. The upfront payment is basically a loan on your future sales. After you receive the first check, you'll most likely get a royalty deal, which is usually five to ten percent of the books cover price. For the most part, this isn't a business for the lazy, but if you're willing to grind it out then you'll ball outta control!

ACQUISITIONS

Acquisition is when the publishers decide to buy your book. Publishing houses are all in competition to see who can buy the best manuscripts. They mostly rely on agents to supply them with good product. Once an agent convinces an editor to read your product, you've passed a major hurdle. If your book is well written and the editor likes it, then, and only then, you'll enter the process of acquisition.

Every publisher has a committee dedicated to finding the best manuscripts. Their main goal is to find a product that will make their company the most money. This committee consists of editors, publishers, sales and marketing representatives. These committees base their decisions on a criterion that includes three basic things, and they are as follows:

1. Whether or not they feel that the product is well written and entertaining.

2. Whether or not the book will attract enough readers to turn a profit.

3. Whether the subject matter is promotable or not. Do people care about what you wrote about?

If your book doesn't meet all three of these, the truth of the matter is that you just won't make the cut. And, yes, timing is essential when you're working with the big publishing houses. Publishers like to keep their book lists well rounded. If they already bought three other books on the same subject you wrote about then chances are you won't make the cut. Your book might be better than the ones they already bought, but since they came first, you're out of luck. This might not be the case if you go straight through a publisher who works with urban novels because that is their publishing expertise, but that's how it works when you're going through the larger publishing houses.

If your book has met all of their criteria then you'll reach the next level; that's when they'll make you an offer.

THE MEETING

So, you made it past the haters and entered the realm of the publishers. You should always keep in mind that some of these larger publishing houses release 100's and thousands of books a year, so if you want your product to get any extra attention, you'll have to make your presence known. Hopefully they'll like you enough to be motivated to push your product to the utmost of their ability.

What you need to do first is set up a meeting with the editor and ask him to invite all the members of the team that will be involved in publishing your work. Chances are, they won't grant you this request, but if they do, that'll tell you how important you are to their company. Plus, you gotta take into consideration that if you don't got a cell phone where you can facetime with these people, there are all kinds of hoops they have to hop through just to get you parole agent or counselor to fix something like this up. The only way you're gonna get one of these major companies to start catering to you is to write some hitters. Once they see that fucking with you is worth some money, you'll be able to start calling some shots.

Once you sign the contract to sell your book you lose your rights. The book now belongs to the publishers. Therefore, if you want your ideas heard you'll have to kick up some dust. If you come off as respectable person who knows what he's talking about they'll be more apt to listen to your ideas.

EDITING

The urban novel industry is flooded with so much product that books that need a lot of editing don't even make it past the initial screening. Before you send the book to anyone it should be cleaned of any clerical errors. If it's not, it probably won't make it past that assistant I was telling you about earlier.

Most of the time an editor will only request a minor rewrite, and it's your job to meet all the deadlines they set for you. The copyrights will always be yours, but since you sold your rights to the publisher the editor is now your boss. Make sure you stay cool with the editor, because he or she will be your contact within this conglomerate.

SCHEDULING

It usually takes two years from the time of your acquisition to the date of your book release. It all depends on the subject matter and when your publisher believes your book will sell the most. It also depends on the completion and how many books your publisher already has on the subject you wrote about. This is why it's so important to meet your deadlines, because you don't want to mess up what your publishers have in mind. Missing a deadline by a week can basically delay your book release for another year. It will also affect your reputation, because no one wants to work with someone who can't be depended upon.

NUMBERS

During the acquisition process the publisher is already crunching numbers. They figure out how many books need to be sold to make everyone a profit. Profitability affects everything they do regarding the publication of your urban novel. These numbers will dictate how much attention they'll give your book, so you need to ask for your "budget numbers." The publishers don't usually tell these numbers to the author, but if you do get your hands on this information, it'll give you an idea of how serious this project is to them.

PRODUCTION

What's really real is that readers do judge a book by its cover. This is the part where the publishers shine the most. They all have a production department who is in charge of the designs on the cover and the interior of the book, along with the printing and the binding of the finished product.

The good thing about being involved in the publication process is that you'll know when the production department will get ahold of your book. This means that you'll know when you can talk to them about your cover design. As long as you don't come off like you're trying to run things, and you submit your ideas in advance, chances are they'll let you speak your mind. If you happen to have unique ideas you might become an asset. However, if you come off like you're the boss when you really aren't, they aren't gonna fuck wit' you. It's all on you and your social game. Don't forget, you sold your rights, so in all actuality, they really don't have to listen to anything you've got to say.

MARKETING

There are three major parts to marketing, and they are as follows:

1. Advertisement; this includes paid ads of your book in magazines or on the internet.

2. Promotion; that is anything that promotes your book, from posters to free hat giveaways.

3. Publicity; anything that draws attention to you as the author, or your book.

The more publicity your book gets, the more of a chance that people will go out and buy your book. It's as simple as that.

Marketing works the best when you have a team that knows how to apply the right amount of advertisement, promotion, and publicity. There's no specific time in the process of publication when you should start or stop the marketing. You should automatically be prepared to be actively involved in the process, from beginning to end.

SALES

Every publishing house has a sales department. It's their job to not only figure out what season it should be released, but they also contact all the big chain booksellers like Barnes & Noble and Amazon.com. This way they can sell your books to them months in advance. They also get at independent booksellers, but chances are your book will be sold to targeted markets, so don't worry if you wrote an urban novel based in LA and it doesn't get released in New York. Your sales team will usually release your book in a set area just to see how good it sells. If the sales are strong, they'll release it in another part of the country, then another, until your book is being read by people from coast to coast.

At first, the number of books released to these stores won't be too high, but don't stress off this either. The object is to have the bookseller's sell out of your product so they'll have to buy more. If they sell out then they'll know you're a money maker. When you write another book, they'll be quick to buy those, too.

Once your book is finally being sold then you've reached your goal. You've become an established writer. So now you know the business, and the better you are at business the higher you'll climb the ranks.

CHAPTER TWENTY

Rejection

I just walked you through the business aspect of this industry as if it was extremely easy to get a book deal. I want to get it out in the open right now, though; getting a book deal is nowhere as easy as I just made it sound. Most writers go years before getting a book deal, but they never give up, no matter how many people tell 'em it won't happen. I'm one of those people who wouldn't give up, and my back was against a wall. There was a time when I didn't have the support system that I have now. If you know anything about The Cell Block's history you know that I had to actually send my book into the prison system (from the streets) to get it published. But don't take my story as a gauge... Stephen King received something like 125 rejections before he ever got a chance to show the world his skills, and look at him now. He's one the highest paid novelist of all time.

The main things is you shouldn't give up after receiving a few rejection letters. What you need to do is turn every loss into a win. Instead of letting a fall make you quit, let that fall make you stronger.

See, most of the time if you send a SASE with your query letter, you'll receive some kind of feedback as to why you were denied. I know your first instinct is to probably throw away any such letter, but what you need to do is study the excuse they gave you. Use it to better yourself and any project you are working on. Sometimes they'll even tell you how you can fix what you've already written.

Here's a few responses you might get when a company is trying to shoot you to the curb:

- **No Response:** If you don't get a response and you know for a fact that you sent a SASE, then forget 'em! It's their loss. You don't want to deal with a company that doesn't have the decency to let you know what you did wrong.
- **Form Rejection:** Sometimes you'll receive a standardized letter which is kinda impersonal, but don't take it that way, it just means the editor who sent it is swamped with work. This is the most common form of rejection, so don't trip.
- **Personalized Rejection:** This can come in many different forms, from a handwritten letter to a neatly written missive explaining why they didn't want your urban novel. This is actually a good rejection because they are showing you that they cared enough to get at you in detail. You really should take whatever advice they send and then resubmit your manuscript. Just make sure to send it back with a copy of the letter they sent to you.
- **Rejection With an Invitation to Resubmit:** Now, this is what you really want (other than an actual acceptance). If you receive this type of rejection, you better hurry up and fix whatever they mentioned and send it back ASAP! But, when you do send it back, send it with a copy of their letter.
- **Acceptance:** This might come in a phone call to one of your free world contacts, but if not, you'll get a letter. And when you get an acceptance it's time to cop you some pruno and a stick of that sticky-icky and start celebrating. Your dreams have finally materialized.

Here's a few reasons editors might give you for not accepting your work:

"Not our style": Basically, they're saying your work is good, but they don't publish urban novels. Don't trip, just try another company.

"We're not accepting new clients": This is a good sign that this house is going out of business. Go ahead and try another company.

"This topic is played out": Publishers try to keep their subject matter spread out, so they might already have too many books on that specific subject. This doesn't mean your work isn't any good, it's just that they already have too many titles in that subject. Find a way to switch up your content a little so that you won't receive the same response from another publishing house.

"We only publish authors with platforms": Some publishing companies are so small that they do not have the money in their budget to promote their projects. This means they will only publish authors with their own clientele or fan base. If you didn't mention anything in your query letter about a fan base or platform, they'll just discard your submission. Create a platform. A platform can be anything from a personal website to a Facebook page; anything. After you do this then add it in your next query letter for the next company.

"You didn't identify your theme": You obviously didn't identify your theme. Your work is probably too broad to even be considered an urban novel. You're gonna need someone to look at your work, and give you some constructive criticism. If you've received more than one reply like this, chances are, you're gonna need to rewrite your whole book.

"Like your protagonist, but we can't represent you": They're basically saying that you are good at creating characters, but you're lacking in other areas like dialogue, plot, or conflict. You're probably gonna need someone else to look at your work, because you might need some help in one of the aspects of craft.

"Numerous grammatical errors:" This means you either didn't proof-read your work, or you have too many spelling errors. Now, come on, man! If you sent your urban novel without proofreading it then you deserve a rejection! Go sign up for an English class or something.

"The book didn't excite me": If you received a letter like this then they must have asked you to send them the rest of your urban novel after reading the first few chapters and they just didn't like it. All that means is that you started off strong and got weaker towards the end. What you need to do is reread your work. Where did you lose focus? Did you waiver from p.o.v.? Did the action slow down? Find it, fix it.

"This isn't something we publish, but did you try so and so?": This is one of the better rejections, because they are telling you that you have some good work. For them to actually recommend another company means they really like your book, but they don't publish urban novels. What you need to do is contact the editor of the recommended company and tell him/her who recommended you then ask them if you can send 'em your query letter. Then get ahold of the last company and thank them.

There are many forms of rejection, but you have to learn how to recognize constructive criticism and capitalize on it. However, if you have no patience, and you really want to make things happen, maybe you should look into self-publishing.

CHAPTER TWENTY-ONE

Self-Publishing

I just walked you through the traditional route of how to get your urban novel published. Then I topped it off with a whole chapter dedicated solely to rejection. The reason I did that is because 99% of all query letters get rejected, especially when you're writing these kinds of books. There aren't many publishing houses that work on urban novels. Nevertheless, if you do your homework, you will find some that do specialize in this genre. In the following pages there'll be a whole section dedicated to give you every address you may want to look into regarding getting your work published.

If you go through every company that publishes urban novels and you still don't get a deal, then chances are, you won't.

At this point you need to ask yourself this question: Is your book any good? Maybe it's garbage. Then again, maybe it isn't. If you really believe in yourself then you gotta do you! In the last decade the norm has been changed, and that's been proven by the multitudes who go straight to the internet with their products and become rich and famous. Other than the fact that you're in a prison cell, why can't you win like the rest of 'em? Shiiit, Mike Enemigo created The Cell Block while he's been in prison, and now he's got us all eating.

I've set up a questionnaire for you to take a look at before deciding to self-publish. I hope that it helps you in your decision-making process.

1. Is there anything I should take into consideration before I decide to self-publish?

Yes!

QUALITY: You never want to self-publish without editing your work. It's better to hire a professional to do this. A lot of times writers fall in love with their work, so they shy away from taking out the parts that should be discarded. Most companies won't edit your work unless you pay an extra fee. But, the fact that you're in prison and can't get money like you want to can make your funds limited. So, why not just take your time, or find you a legal beagle who knows about grammar to take a look at your shit?

SALES AND DISTRIBUTION: Self-publishing companies make most of their money off you. Traditional publishing houses invest their own money, so they have to make sales just to break even. That means that a traditional publishing house has to hustle to get paid. That's why they have a sales department whose sole purpose is to contact booksellers and push your product.

Without promotion and marketing no one is going to know your product exist. If you don't have a platform of your own you're not gonna sell too many books. You might sell some to an auntie or a cousin, but that ain't shit.

COVER DESIGN AND PACKAGING: People do judge books by their cover. Once you make a book deal with a company their production team is dedicated to coming up with an eye catcher. If you take a look inside of any book from the table of contents to chapter headings and pictures, nothing is done by chance. They have a paid team that comes up with the best ideas for each targeted audience. Self-publishers usually offer one size fits all type templates which offers convenience and economic efficiency, while also making it harder for your book to look unique when it's on the shelf of a book store.

2. After self-publishing, will I still have a chance with traditional publishers?

Hell Yeah!

You can always contact publishers with your work, even if it's already self-published. Even Mike Enemigo has done it with his book *Conspiracy Theory*. This should be your ultimate goal, but here's the catch: If you've already put out a product that doesn't sell, why would a publisher want to put any more money into it? If it does sell well, and you can prove this, then now you have something to work with.

If you've already self-published, you need to get some feet on the streets to help promote your shit. That's where building a network comes in handy. If you read my pen pal book, I explain all that. It's already hard enough for anyone in prison to accomplish the impossible. That's why it's so important that you get some females on the team. You need someone who can fuck with social media to help create a fan base for you. Not only will your numbers show that your product is good, but you'll be stacking bread at the same time. Self-publishing does give you the opportunity to make a lot of money off a little investment, but you gotta work for it. It takes long hours and getting up off your ass every day, but you already should know that nothing worth having comes free in this life.

That's about it for now. I recommend that you keep this book on your shelf and reread it a few times so that you can make sure that you didn't miss anything. Even though I wrote this book, I still read it and use the game I've laced it with. So, good luck, and I look forward to reading all the urban novels that were inspired by this manual.

Positive Energy Always Creates Elevation,
That's PEACE!
King Guru

A REALLY SIMPLE WAY TO GET RICH!

By: Unknown

There is one simple way to get rich. From day one, you could have over one million dollars in less than a year.

This is really simple, but it is not easy. It will require some work.

Here is the method. You will find, or develop a product that many persons want. It must be inexpensive to produce, and it must provide a large profit margin.

Using an example is the best way to tell you how this method works. In the early 1970's, I read about a book that told how a lazy man could get rich. The book sold for $10.

At the time, $10 was a lot of money. You could buy a full-size automobile for a little over $2,000.

Since I have never been fond of work, I decided I needed a copy of this book. So, I scraped together $10 and ordered the book.

For my $10, I received a book about how to make money in mail order. It did contain some good mail order information, but it did not tell how a lazy man could get rich.

A lot of people were conned, just as I was. The author sold over 1,000,000 copies at $10 each. He invested a lot that money in advertising, but he still put several million dollars in his pocket.

That one book was his only product. He did not try to get any repeat sales orders for other products. He just continued investing his profits in more advertising. For a short time, his ads appeared all over the place. Then he abruptly quit advertising.

I guess his sales started to fall off, and he decided it was time to quit and enjoy his money.

To use this method, all you need is one basic $10 and at least 1,000,000 customers. Invest your profits until sales start to fall off. Then start living the good life.

Several years after I purchased the book, I read that the author was bankrupt at the time he wrote the book. He borrowed money to print the first copies and to run his first ads. Of course, in his advertising, he didn't say that he was bankrupt. He actually claimed that he was wealthy, and he wanted to tell other people how to get rich. He especially wanted to tell lazy people how to get rich.

P.T. Barnum said there is a sucker born every minute. Boy, was he ever wrong. He should have said a hundred suckers every second.

With good advertising, you can sell cow manure and get rich. Believe me, that has already been done.

Some people have made tons of money selling chicken manure. Other persons have made a lot of money with rabbit manure. One man made millions selling ordinary rocks!

The lazy man's wealth building book did provide some good information, even if the author didn't tell the truth about his financial status. The book wasn't manure.

If other people can get rich with this method, so can you. You will have to work hard for a year or two. Then you'll be rich, and you can quit...

CONCLUSION

Now you've gotten the knowledge to write a best seller, but all that means is that your journey is just beginning. Getting a book done and published is hard work. Especially in prison where the cards are stacked against you. If I had to critique myself, I'd say one of the major reasons I am where I am is my work ethic. I don't quit. I don't let obstacles stop me from accomplishing my goals.

Throughout my other writings I've talked about having a Free Dome. To me, a Free Dome is having Freedom, being free. Writing gives me that. Yes, these folks took over a decade to smack me with a life sentence for a cold case. If California doesn't pass these laws that everyone is talking about I'm most likely gonna spend the rest of my life in captivity. That's the T.R.U.T.H., but it's not my reality.

The only prison that can truly hold a real (Original) man is a prison of the mind. And, even people on the streets can do life sentences in that type of prison. One of the ways I combat my situation is by writing. The way I see it is when I wrote *How To Hustle And Win: Sex, Money, Murder Edition*, I was on a Caribbean island at the top of my game. I was overlooking the ocean, with a bad bitch blowing trees in the background. Well, that's where I'm at whenever I'm writing. I'm not here, in this prison cell.

I'm free. So, if you can reach that level of over standing you will be free, too. All you have to do is love what you're doing. Don't look at it like its work, yet dedicate yourself to it as if your life depends on it.

In the following pages you'll find a gang of resources from book publishers to self-publishing companies geared towards prisoners. Get at 'em, get at all of them. And don't be lazy, either. Don't just write a few sentences on half sheets of paper. Get at these companies wholeheartedly. Write every single one, tell them who you are, and make them believe in you! There's one spot I recommend that each and every one of you get at. It's called PrisonsFoundation.Org. It's located in Washington D.C. It's a company/website that publishes prisoner's books for free. It doesn't matter what you write about, your manuscript doesn't even have to be typed! You can submit a whole book written in your very own handwriting. They'll scan it as-is and post it on their website for the world to read for free. I know this 'cuz I fucks' wit' 'em! I already have 2 books published on that site.

The purpose of that site is to get your work out there. If it generates enough buzz you might get noticed by an editor, or an agent, and they'll put you on. Real talk! That's not the only plus to it, either. For those of you who know how to network, those of you who do the pen pal thing on a sophisticated level, having a book in print is a trophy. Whenever you meet someone new, you can send them there to see the type of work you do.

Two of my baby mammas got back on the team after they found out I published a book on that site. I'm telling you, there are people in the free-world who are just looking for a reason to help you do something for yourself, you just have to show initiative. By authoring a book, you are doing just that.

Before I end this I want to write about one more aspect of the prison game. Mike Enemigo's book with Josh Kruger, *The Millionaire Prisoner*, is a must-read for all prison entrepreneurs. The information/ perspective it gives is unique and motivating. It'll keep you grounded, which is important when the money starts coming (and it will start flowing); you need to have your mind right.

One of the first things I see all new money do is start buying gifts for people. They also start buying shit they've always wanted, which isn't that bad until they start spending too much money on shit they don't need. I think all convicts/hustlers should read that book because it breaks down the right mindset to have when moves are being made from the inside of your prison cell.

And, last, but not least; it's in man's nature to see the next man doing something and automatically feel like you can do it better. The other day I was hitting laps with some of my niggaz and we were building on this subject in the cipher. It's a trip because me and the homey, Bolo, were just talking about the same thing earlier that day. Anyways, after everyone listened, spoke, and contemplated the subject matter the consensus was understood to be that, yes, most people do think they can do things better than the next man. B.U.T., what's really real is the people who actually manifest what their mouth speaks.

The next man might be able to write a book that's better than yours. He may have the knowledge of craft down to a science, and have an authentic story to tell; but does he have the drive to put his words on paper? Is he willing to put in the work to make his dreams become a reality? Will he take the time to study the business and network outside of the cell? Probably not. And, that's why you're gonna win. That's why you're the one who'll put a book out, and he'll be the one critiquing you! In this game, just like all the others, it's all about your grind! Never give up! Never stop! Never take NO (Now Cipher) for an answer! Ultimately, you are the sun of your universe, so shine your light and make something grow!

Positive Energy Always Creates Elevation,
That's PEACE!
King Guru

ABOUT THE AUTHOR

King Guru is the author of a number of books including the *Devils & Demons* series; *How To Hustle & Win: Sex, Money, Murder Edition*; and *Pretty Girls Love Bad Boys: The Prisoner's Guide to Getting Girls; B.M.F.;* and *Raw Law For Prisoners.* He is the father of five, and is serving a life sentence in the California Department of Corrections. Guru spent most of his life as an underworld, street entrepreneur and has now channeled his energies into writing urban novels and self-help manuals for convicts and block bleeders.

For contact information and/or correspondence, King Guru can be contacted via facebook@ Wilberto Guru Belardo, or by email: wilbertogurubelardo@gmail.com.

8 URBAN FICTION AUTHORS WHO OVERCAME PRISON AND FORGED LUCRATIVE CAREERS

[By Evette Brown]

These former incarcerated authors turned their sentences into real-life experiences for millions of readers...

Dominating the *Essence* and *New York Times* bestsellers lists, respectively, street literature, officially recognized as urban fiction, has evolved into a permanent part of American literature. Telling the often-tragic stories of African-American men trapped in the gritty realities of urban culture and the women who love them and become victims of vicious cycles, these novels have captivated many in the black community and beyond.

With the success of street literature, many African-American authors have been transformed from street-savvy hustlers to literary inspirations and millionaires. Most of these prominent urban authors are using their life experiences to fuel their passion and words. Here, we feature eight urban authors who were once or are still incarcerated. They all have criminal histories, but now their experiences are used to prevent others from following down such a despairing path.

Wahida Clark

With the release of her 2005 acclaimed debut novel, *Thugs and the Women who Love Them*, the world was introduced to an emerging talent in urban fiction, Wahida Clark. The "Queen on Thug Love Fiction" immediately built a dedicated foundation of readers that were mesmerized with her depictions of a lifestyle that involved hustling, murder, and millions. Writing about the realities of the "ghetto," where loyalty is more valuable than life, Clark used her words to create a literary empire.

Though the New Jersey native is one of the most popular authors writing street literature, for most of her Essence Bestselling career, she was once incarcerated in a women's federal camp in Lexington, Kentucky. After reading a small portion of Shannon Holmes' *B-More Careful* in *XXL* magazine, Clark made the conscious decision to dedicate the remainder of her nine-year-sentence to creating the "Thug" series, thus sharing her experiences in life with the world. Since her release, Wahida Clark had used her position in literature to expose other urban authors to her audience. She is now the head of W. Clark Publishing and is now regarded as a savvy business woman and wise entrepreneur.

Kwame Teague

When *True to the Game* author, Teri Woods, discovered Kwame Teague in a North Carolina prison, a dynasty was created. Serving two life sentences for the shooting deaths of two men (he plead not guilty), Teague refused to spend his time idly, waiting for a possible release date in the future. Instead, he has penned the series, *Dutch*, a wildly successful urban fiction masterpiece that has captured the attention of many readers. Though Kwame's name is not included on the covers of any of the *Dutch* novels for legal reasons, he is the mastermind behind the words. The *Dutch* series has been banned in all state prisons for inciting violence among inmates, but that has not stopped Teague from continuing to write about these fictional characters living real-life situations.

K'wan

K'wan is one of the most accomplished authors in urban fiction, but in 2002, he was merely a novice in the writing world, as he was the first author in line to be published by the relatively small and widely unknown company, Triple Crown Publications. Catching the writing bug while serving a short stint in jail, K'wan was literally dared to write the beginnings of the classic, *Gangsta*. It became the foundation from which Triple Crown Publications was built and evolved into an Essence bestseller and a favorite of many devoted urban fiction readers. Now, with over 10 bestsellers under his belt, a multi-book deal with St. Martin's Press, and thousands of his adoring fans that read whatever he chooses to write, K'wan is regarded as one of the leaders in the genre.

Kiki Swinson

Author of the extremely popular and successful *Wifey* series, Kiki Swinson is a living testament to the resilience of the human spirit. The Portsmouth, Virginia, writer discovered her passion for penning real-life experiences in novel form when she completed her first book, *Mad Shambles*, while serving five-years in federal prison for allegedly being the *"wifey"* of a very successful drug dealer. After being released, Swinson self-published *Mad Shambles* before pitching *Wifey* to publishing houses. Eventually, the book was picked up by Melodrama Publishing and after a sequel, Swinson delivered with *I'm Still Wifey*, *Life After Wifey*, and *Still Wifey Material* along with other popular novels. Fifteen years after being released from prison, Kiki Swinson's life as a narcotics kingpen's wifey had generated a hefty profit.

Shannon Holmes

Bronx, New York native, Shannon Holmes, was armed with nothing more than a GED and a prison record when he decided that writing about his street experiences rather than living them was his life's mission. While serving five years in prison for various drug convictions, Holmes wrote his first novel and negotiated a deal with Triple Crown Publications. His timely classic, *B-More Careful*, was the launching pad for his successful career as an author. Going on to sell half-a-million copies, *B-More Careful* transformed Holmes into a platinum commodity in publishing. After negotiating a two-book, six-figure deal with Simon and Schuster, Holmes continues to be a giant in urban fiction. His softmore novel, *Bad Girlz* sold 50,000 copies in the first week alone and he accomplished a feat that no other urban fiction author had been able to do in the past. His critically acclaimed book, *Never Go Home Again* was the first in the genre to be printed in hardcover. Now crowned as the "King of Hip-Hop Literature," Holmes has negotiated a larger deal with St. Martin's Press and released several other popular street novels.

Jihad

Seven years in federal prison served Jihad well. It awakened his conscious to the issues plaguing the African-American community and inspired him to begin writing and using his experiences to motive others to achieve the impossible. After signing a deal with Envisions Publishing, Jihad created the Jihad Uhuru Wake-Up Everybody Foundation and began creating thought-provoking characters for his popular novels, including *Preacherman Blues, Preacherman Blues 2,* and *Baby Girl*. As an award-winning novelist and *Essence* bestseller, Jihad is nine novels into his blossoming career and is in the process of adapting *Baby Girl* into a screenplay.

Vickie M. Stringer

All hail the Queen of Hip-Hop Literature! Vickie M. Stringer is a literary powerhouse. After founding the renowned publishing company Triple Crown Publications, Stringer was integral in changing the publishing world by creating a stable of urban authors with powerful stories to share with the world. Once considered the "Cocaine Queen" of Columbus, Ohio, Stringer served seven years in federal prison before realizing that she had a knack and passion for writing. After her release, stringer found Triple Crown Publications. After receiving 26 rejection letters from different publishing houses, Stringer self-published *Let That Be the Reason*, selling it out the trunk of her car at salons and barbershops. Now, she has inked a deal with Simon & Schuster to publish her successful novels including *Dirty Red* while she still seeks talent for her Triple Crown Publications, which is rumored to be worth millions. Vickie M. Stringer turned her life into a living testament to the power of determination, strong will, and the resilience of the human spirit.

Treasure Hernandez

There isn't much known about one of Kensington Publishing Corporation's premiere authors, Treasure Hernandez, but her novels are a grim slice of urban reality. As the creator of the *Flint* and *Baltimore Chronicles* series, Hernandez is a force to be reckoned with in the urban fiction genre. After her words were discord by fellow author, Carl Weber, Hernandez has been in a tunnel headed towards success. The most powerful aspect of Treasure Hernandez' journey is that she is currently incarcerated, but has released a full seven-book series, three books of a new series, and two other independent novels. Once she is released, Treasure will be able to capitalize on the career that she has established behind prison walls.

INTERVIEW WITH DUTCH

By Mike Enemigo

Iceberg Slim is credited with creating the street lit genre with his 1967 autobiography *Pimp: The Story of My Life*, and though he sold over 6 million books before his death in 1992, it was Donald Goines who really ran with the genre. Goines, after learning about Iceberg Slim's book *Pimp* while serving time in prison, penned his semi-autobiographical novel *Whoreson*, which was published in 1972 by Iceberg Slim's publisher, Holloway House. Goines would then go on to write 17 books, all detailing the sex, drugs, murder, and other elements of the Black underworld, before he was brutally murdered on October 21, 1974, in a style much like you'd read in one of his books.

After Goines's murder, with the exception of a few books by Iceberg Slim before his 1992 death, the street lit genre largely remained dormant until around 1999, when Sister Souljah dropped what would become one of the greatest street lit books of all time, *The Coldest Winter Ever*. This reignited the street lit genre, and soon-to-be publishing powerhouse Teri Woods began looking for talent. She would find this talent inside a prison cell in a North Carolina prison, and together they would release one of the greatest street lit series of all time: *Dutch*. Soon, the genre would be crowning a new king: North Carolina prisoner Kwame Teague, aka Dutch.

I recently had the opportunity to tap in with Dutch, from my prison cell in California to his in North Carolina, where we discussed the past, present, and future of the game.

Mike: Dutch, my guy, thanks for agreeing to interview with me, I know you don't do this a lot. Just for those who don't know, introduce yourself, tell us where you're from.

Dutch: I'm Kwame Teague, I go by Dutch. I'm from Newark, New Jersey, but I've been incarcerated in North Carolina since 1994.

What was life like growing up in Newark, New Jersey?

Growing up in Newark, in the 80s, I saw the transition of the Black community, culture and economy change with the explosion of hip-hop. The youth took over the music, fashion, and identity. The community began to change because of the AIDS epidemic, as well as the Democratic party's total embrace of identity politics – a game they've been using on us ever since. Lastly, the crack game broke us down economically. It also gave us the opportunity to rebuild, we just squandered it.

How'd you end up in North Carolina from New Jersey?

I came to North Carolina primarily to get involved in the music scene. I was managing two rappers and I felt we could get a deal easier in North Carolina than up north in New York, New Jersey, or Pennsylvania, because they were already saturated with it. And we did end up getting a deal for my group Brik Flava through Funhouse Records. The record "Bossman" is still on the Internet.

What did you ultimately get locked up for?

Kidnapping and murder.

That's crazy. My prison has its own channel where they show all kinds of educational and informational stuff. I just saw an interview with a guy named David Jassy. David is from Sweden. He came up in the 80s, started rappin', and eventually songwriting. About 10 years ago he came to California to write for Britney Spears, and while at a crosswalk, got in a fight, killing a man. He was sentenced to 15-to-Life. He eventually got to San Quentin where they have all kinds of programs. He came up on a keyboard, where he was ultimately granted permission to facilitate a "hip-hop class." They produced *The San Quentin Mixtape Project*, which got a distribution deal with Roc Nation. One day, he performed his song "Freedom" at a TED event the prison had, and our governor, Gavin Newsom was in the audience. Governor Newson ultimately pardoned David; he was in Dubai, on business, while his interview was conducted over Zoom. I don't know the details of your case, and I don't want to, but it made me think of this – on business for music and getting convicted of murder. But David is out now, doing big things. Point is, it ain't ever over, you feel me?

Naw, it's never over. I'm very hopeful about my future. And I didn't know about David Jassy and *The San Quentin Mixtape Project*, that's a dope story.

So how did you get the name Dutch?

The name Dutch just comes from the title of the book. I named it *Dutch* because I mistakenly thought Dutch was a title of royalty. So, the tagline was: "There Are Princes... There Are Kings... And then there's Dutch." People just started calling me Dutch after that and it stuck.

What got you into writing? How and when did it start?

I got started at an early age, when my older sister Sharon taught me how to write movie scripts. I was attracted to the format – it was so clean and organized. Anyone who has seen a movie script will know what I mean. This was in the 80s.

Who or what inspires you when it comes to writing?

Movies. I love movies. Especially old movies like *Casablanca* and *Maltese Falcon*. I love the witty dialogue. And Donald Goines has been a big inspiration, too. Iceberg Slim was mean, but Donald was a better storyteller.

What gave you the idea to write the *Dutch* series?

The idea basically comes from Newark. The Dutch character, his whole swag, is made up of several major players from Newark that I grew up hearing about.

How did you end up connecting with Teri Woods?

I read about her in a *Vibe* magazine and had my people contact her.

There are a lot of rumors she does foul business. Is this true? Was this your experience?

Without a doubt, Teri and I have had our differences. But no more than what typically goes on in this industry. Whenever your talent is the commodity, the producer/publisher/financer is going to make moves. Like the old saying goes, "You don't get what you're worth, you get what you negotiate." My second deal was better than my first because I learned my worth and how to negotiate. We were all new and just learning at this time. We're good, though. I'm still in contact with her.

Why do you think *Dutch* was so successful?

I think it was largely based on timing. It was the beginning of the street lit game, aside from Iceberg Slim and Donald Goines, of course, and me, Teri, and Shannon Holmes were able to capitalize on that by being the pioneers.

Do you think that type of success is still possible today?

I think so, but it would take opening up new markets, like Canada, the UK, Germany, etc., where it's not so oversaturated. And probably by appealing to this new generation with audio books, an idea I know you want to take to the next level.

What do you think is the major difference between then and now?

The game then was pre social media and pre music streaming, etc. Now everything is on your phone, and there's so much "right now, at your fingertips" entertainment, it's harder to get people to read. And because the game is so oversaturated, it's harder to make a name now.

I feel you. I've been in the game for 10 years and I'm barely getting a name in the street lit market. I'd been gettin' all my pennies with my how-to and prisoner-info books for prisoners. That's one market that does still read – prisoners – since they don't have access to all the same entertainment and Information options that everyone on the outside has.

Absolutely. There's still some money in these prisons for sure.

So, after Teri, you began publishing your books with DC Book Diva. How'd that come about?

I connected with DC Book Diva – Juanita Short – through a mutual friend. We hit it off immediately because she's so driven, sincere, and she's one of the smartest women I know. And she's gorgeous, too. (Laughs) She is a true diva.

Have you ever tried to get published by a mainstream publishing house that publishes street lit, like St. Martin's Press, who publishes folks like JaQuavis Coleman?

Naw, I never tried to connect with a mainstream publisher because I believe in building our own. I used to preach to other authors all the time that we need to create our own industry, combine our resources, join forces, etc., but our people are so distrustful of each other, and most haven't learned to get past that.

How come you never started your own publishing company?

I just never really had the team for that, to be honest.

I recently saw you did a comic book with Seth Ferranti. How'd you connect with Seth?

Seth and I began writing each other when he was in the feds. I reached out to him and we've been rocking together ever since.

Yeah, Seth is official. I'd even go as far as to say he kinda pioneered street lit journalism, at least as far as books go. I mean, you had magazines like *Don Diva* and *FEDS*, but he took it to the next level with his *Street Legend* books, books about Supreme, Fat Cat, Rich Porter, etc. I know he's who got me into the street lit journalism books. And

now he's really doin' boss shit with his *White Boy* documentary on STARZ. Shout out to Seth, for sure.

Yeah, Seth is official. He's doin' his thing.

What do you think about the comic book game?

The comic book/graphic novel game is wide open, but no one has really mastered it yet. I mean, a gangsta-ass comic book has major potential, but it has to have the right appeal – you gotta know how to push it just right. Seth and I are always kickin' ideas, but we haven't initiated anything new yet.

How would you describe your writing style?

I'd say it's more of a straightforward style. I don't do the long, drawn out details. I like to skip the parts that bog down the story. I have a cinematic style.

What do you think are your best books?

I'd have to say *Dynasty 3* and *Dutch 2: Angel's Revenge*. They have the most interesting storylines in my opinion.

What are your top three books written by others?

My favorite writer, hands down, is Al-Saadiq Banks. He brings that Newark shit hard and his stories are realistic. But my favorite three books are *Block Party 3* by Al-Saadiq Banks, *Cheetah* by Missy Jackson, and *Flight* by Tamara John.

That's crazy you mention Al-Saadiq because I be tellin' people the same thing. I write about this in my upcoming book, *Jailhouse Publishing*. When I had online access, I would watch his videos on IG where he would explain his experiences with the writing game — the struggles he

MIKE ENEMIGO & KING GURU

went through, and how he got past it. I tapped in with him and he fucked with me. And just to keep it real, though I had known who he was, of course, I had yet to read one of his books at the time. But he became my favorite street lit author just based on *him*, you feel me? Based on the authenticity I felt from his videos and tappin' in with him. I then bought *Caught 'em Slippin*, and indeed, it didn't disappoint. It was raw. He really writes that "True 2 Life" shit, you feel me? Shout out to Al-Saadiq Banks.

Yeah, Al-Saadiq Banks is the truth for real.

What is something you've learned since writing your first book?

I've learned that not everyone can see your vision, so you have to believe in yourself enough to stay committed.

Fa sho. And give us some game: What's the secret to success, yours or otherwise?

The secret is total commitment to the vision. Stay open-minded and receptive to advice and critique, but be aware enough to see through the hate.

What advice would you give to someone who wants to do what you do?

My advice is to organize, network, reflect, implement. Organize your thoughts until they become concrete plans, then network to move the plan forward, gaining allies and resources. Reflect on your progress, your mistakes, your missed opportunities, and them implement the next phase. Then, starting from organization again, repeat.

What's a typical day like for you?

A typical day for me is, I get up at 4:30 am, shower, collect my thoughts, listen to NPR News, and read the paper. I plot out my day — the calls I need to make, stuff I need to do, etc. Then I go to work as a graphic designer until 11:00 am, and at that time I have lunch, use the phone, and maybe network a little until 12:00, when I go back to work until 3:30. After 3:30 I might use the phone a little more, write, watch the news, then go to bed around 11:00. I wake up the next day and repeat.

There are rumors you're getting into the movie business. Any truth to this?

Movies are my future. The movie *DUTCH* comes out December 24 [2020]. I'm mad hyped to finally see my shit on screen, even though I didn't write the script for this one. I did write the scripts for parts two and three, though. I'm looking for actors and actresses who believe in their talent. Get at me!

What is your ultimate goal with writing; movies?

Movies, and I want to own my own TV network and/or streaming service.

I can see it. The folks iHustle at *Street Money* magazine just hit me today and said they started an Apple TV channel, Roku channel, and Amazon Fire channel. I gave him your address and he said he sent you a magazine, too. I think you guys will for sure be able to build.

Anyway, good lookin' on the interview. I'ma get this all type up properly and get it all sent out to everybody. And you already know we're going to cook somethin' up. Mike Enemigo, Dutch. Books, movies. What should we tell 'em about that?

Just tell 'em they should be very afraid. (laughs)

INTERVIEW WITH WAHIDA CLARK

Vice talked to the originator of the street lit fiction genre to discuss how she pioneered a nuanced take on the romance novel from within a federal prison.

Wahida Clark is the reigning O.G. of street lit, also called "urban fiction." Best known for her *Thug* and *Payback* series, Clark writes nuanced takes on the schlocky romance novels you see at grocery stores, replacing the cheese with guns, cash, gangs, and drugs. And Clark isn't just fabricating inner-city tall tales; she's writing about what she's lived through.

Born and bred in the streets of Trenton, New Jersey, Clark was involved with the New World, a crew of black separatist bank robbers known for beheading their rivals, and served time as a result. While doing a sentence of 125 months in federal prison for money laundering and wire fraud, Clark began writing fiction while locked up. She wrote her first book, *Thugs and the Women Who Love Them*, using a pen and yellow legal paper in her cell, but was released from prison in 2007 and has published 14 books in the time since, including *Thuggz Valentine*. In the case of *Thuggz Valentine*, Clark remixed the familiar story of Bonnie and Clyde, but tweaked it so it reflects her own experiences while involved with a real crime syndicate.

After opening her own publishing house, Wahida Clark Presents, she put out 70-plus titles from incarcerated authors like CASH, Victor L. Martin (author of *A Hood Legend*), and others. Clark has also signed deals with major publishing houses like Kensington and Hachette, been hand-picked by Birdman to have her books distributed through Cash Money Records, and is now entering the movie and TV game with Wahida Clark films, which currently has two projects in development based on her *Thug Series*. *Vice* gave Clark a call to talk about her rise in the publishing game from within a jail cell, as well as what she's done since being on the outside.

VICE: How did you get into writing?

Wahida Clark: I started writing while serving my ten-and-a-half-year federal prison sentence. When my back was up against the wall, when I discovered that all my money and possessions were gone, when I discovered that it takes money to live in prison, and when it hit me that I have to do something in order to walk out of prison with a cushion, I prayed for guidance and was blessed to recognize and act on the guidance when it came. The guidance was to write street fiction.

My husband was also locked up and our daughters were teenagers, so I had to somehow get my hustle on. My husband wrote a book called *Uncle Yah Yah* and then I saw a clip about Shannon Holmes, who signed his first book deal in prison, and I said I could do this.

What did your husband say when you told him you also wanted to write a book from inside?

At first, my husband didn't respond. I had to holla at him again and again, saying, "Yo, I'm thinking about writing a book. I'm serious. What do you think?" When he finally got back to me, he said what [publishers] are interested in from people in our position is sex, drugs, murder, and crime. I had experience in that world, and what I didn't experience myself in New Jersey, those around me experienced. I wrote about what I knew.

My husband said if I sent him a little sample, he'd give me his advice. I was working in the prison library and studying the craft, and began writing and sending things to him. On top of his encouragement, as inmate who was previously a literary agent gave a creative writing class, and the rest slowly became history. I was blessed that my time in prison was time well spent.

What was it like to sign a book deal while you were incarcerated?

I signed two deals with two major publishing houses while I was serving time – it was crazy and awesome. I was writing those books with paper and ink, too! I hit the *Essence* magazine best sellers list multiple times while incarcerated. It was such an inspiration to so many sisters and brothers on lock that many of them wrote and told me that I was the reason many of them started writing. I would get letters seeking advice, plus receive words of encouragement from authors who are now publishers and are now moving into film. It was a wonderful thing to inspire others. On top of being a four-time *New York Times* Best Seller, it feels like a wonderful accomplishment.

What separates street lit and the *Thug* series from the typical romance novels that middle-ages suburban moms read?

Two different environments produce two different mindsets. They are the same, but they are seen differently. No one can say there isn't violence in romance novels.

What did you do differently with *Thuggz Valentine*?

Thuggz Valentine is the story of a modern-day Bonnie and Clyde – natural born killers who go out in a blaze of glory after taking on the city's police force. The first thing I did differently was write the book in reverse – it opens with the ending. The second was a collaboration with David Weaver, the King of e-book publishing. We had agreed to do an experiment, so I had him publish the e-book version. Needless to say, it worked out well.

Your *Thug* series is now being turned into a film, right? How far into the process are you?

I'm excited. My fans are excited. Since the series is so popular the producers and directors haven't decided which route to go first: a play, a TV series, or a movie.

We are going to do something. In December, we're having a party/talent search/networking event in Atlanta. We are going to find our direction and our stars there.

Do you have any other film projects in the works?

Blood Heist, written by NuariceArt, hasn't been published under Wahida Clark Presents yet, but the film rights were picked up immediately. It's about Angelo and Michael, two brothers joined in the hunt to take the reins on their father's kingdom.

It's a good look to move into film, a natural progression. I'm a storyteller by nature; that's what I do. I am constantly looking for different mediums to tell my stories. Film is just the latest and it also happens to be the biggest art form. There's a lot of crime drama on TV these days, but if I have my way, God willing, I will clean up the whole industry and make something better.

Do you ever think that glamorizes street lit romanticizes or even crime?

We try our best to follow personal principles and literary principles that demand those good triumphs over evil all the time. However, the demand today is for junk food – both physically and mentally.

My husband taught me that it was easier to write books for money than to write books to educate. So of course, we took the road for money, on hopes that it would put us in position to educate. It's a constant grind and hustle. If you are not constantly pushing your business it will remain stagnate. And of course, content is King. Or, in my case, Queen.

[Source: Vice.com]

URBAN PUNCTUATION GUIDE

APOSTROPHE '

1. Indicates the possessive case of singular and plural nouns, indefinite pronouns, surnames with designations such as Jr. and Sr.:

NOTE: When indicating possession for a plural noun, the apostrophe goes on the outside of the s. Singular nouns already ending in S still need the additional S after the apostrophe.

The gangster's gun	The Bloods' block
My homie's car	The James's new house
Mike's bitch	The Business's location
2013's most valuable player	The Prisons' Wardens

2. Indicates the omission of letters in contractions:

He isn't the one.
I wouldn't've done that.
That's good shit.
I could've made a lot of money with that.

NOTE: It's = it is; its, with no apostrophe, is possessive.

3.   Indicates that letters have intentionally been omitted from the spelling of a word in order to reproduce a perceived pronunciation, or to give an informal flavor to a writing:

That beat is knockin'.
Tell 'im what I said.
Fuck all of 'em.
He knocked yo' ass out.

BRACKETS [ ]

1.   Used to enclose words or passages in quotations to indicate the insertion of material written by someone other than the original writer/speaker:

I went to [the store on] the corner.
We smoked that [weed] right there and got high as fuck.
Fill the entire clip with [hallow point] bullets.

2.   Used to enclose material inserted within material already in parentheses:

I stopped by the house (in Sacramento [CA]) to drop off the guns.

COLON:

1.   Introduces words, phrases, or clauses that explain, amplify, or summarize what has preceded:

Suddenly my reality hit me: I would die in prison.
In prison, a man has two things: his balls and his word.
I had what I needed to settle the score: my shank.

2.   Introduces a list:

I have everything we need for the job: two bulletproof vests, two handguns, two masks and six duffle bags.

NOTE: In uses 1 and 2, a complete sentence should normally precede the colon.

3.   Follows the salutation in a business letter:

Dear Mr. Wright:
To whom it may concern:
Gentlemen:

COMMA,

1.   Separates the clauses of a compound sentence connected by a coordinating conjunction (for, yet, but, so, nor, and, or):

I like his drawings, but I wouldn't let him tattoo on me.
I used to love that girl, and I have no problem admitting it to the world.

NOTE: You can leave the comma out in short compound sentences in which the connection between the clauses are close:

I heard what he said and I didn't like it.
I threatened him with a lawsuit and he backed off.

2.   Separates and/or from the final item in a series of 3 or more:

I got coke, weed, and meth for sale.

I love Nicki Minaj, Beyonce, Kate Upton, and about 999 other bad bitches.

3.   Separates two or more adjectives modifying the same noun when "and" could be used between them without changing the meaning:

A cold, dark prison cell.
A beautiful, intelligent woman.

4.   Sets off a non-restrictive clause (one that if eliminated would not change the meaning of the sentence): The Escalade, which I've owned for years, is cleaner than the Navigator I just bought.

NOTE: The comma should not be used when the clause is restrictive (essential to the meaning of the sentence): The Escalade that is sitting on 26-inch rims is grey with beige leather interior.

5.   Sets off transitional words and short expressions that require a pause in reading or speaking:

Unfortunately, I did not get a visit today.
On the other hand, I was prepared for the pain.
Of course, I would love to get out of prison.

6.   Sets off a subordinate clause or a long phrase that precedes a principal clause:

NOTE: If the subordinate clause follows the independent clause, the comma is usually omitted:

If I ever get out of prison, I will never come back.
After I read the letter, I understood everything she meant.
If I see you first, I'll yell.

I'll yell if I see you first.

7. Sets off words used in direct address:

Thank you, mom, for all that you've done.
Nicki, please send me some pictures of you in a thong.

8. Separates a tag question from the rest of the sentence:

Jessica Alba is a bad bitch, isn't she?
I think Drake's new CD is knockin', don't you?

9. Follows the salutation in a personal letter, and the complimentary close in a business or personal letter:

Dear Ninel,
My dearest love,
Forever yours,
Sincerely,

DASH −

1. Sets apart an explanatory or defining phrase or list:

Some of the most beautiful women in the world − Beyonce, Alicia Keys, Rihanna, Ninel Conde, etc. − are also the wealthiest.
I immediately realized what prison is − hell.

2. Sets apart parenthetical material −

My '68 Malibu − the candy blue one sitting on 22-inch rims − was my favorite car.

NOTE: If you use dashes to set apart an explanatory, defining phrase, list, or parenthetical material in the middle of a sentence, the sentence must also make sense if it were removed:

Some of the most beautiful women in the world are also the wealthiest.
My '68 Malibu was my favorite car.

ELLIPSIS POINTS . . .

1. Indicate, by three spaced points, the omission of words or sentences within quoted matter:

The Playboy Club was established in 1960 ... It's now worth a fortune.

2. Indicate, by four spaced points, the omission of words at the end of a sentence (one for the period, three for the ellipsis points):

Loyalty and respect is a must.... But you would never know it by the actions of these fools.

3. Indicate, by three spaced points, a pause in the middle of a sentence for dramatic effect:

She turned around and saw ... nothing.

4. Indicate, by four spaced points, a pause at the end of a sentence for dramatic effect:

In the end, he turned out to be what I suspected: a rat....

EXCLAMATION POINT!

1. Terminates an emphatic or exclamatory sentence:

I can't believe you!
Fuck you, bitch!

2.   Terminates most interjections:

Ouch! Stop! No way!

HYPHEN -

1.   Indicates that part of a word of more than one syllable has been carried over from one line to the next:

When I go to the yard, I enjoy work-
    ing out on the bars.
You could never fully understand how pain-
    ful prison is unless you've been here.

NOTE: Words can be split only in certain places, usually between syllables – see your dictionary.

2.   Joins the elements of compound modifiers preceding nouns:

That's a well-done tattoo.
It's a two-hour movie.
I hope you pick up game from my letter-writing book.

NOTE: The hyphen is not usually needed when the hyphenated set is not a directly preceding adjective:

The tattoo is well done.
The movie was two hours long.

3.   Punctuates written-out compound numbers from 21 to 99:

I plan to be ballin' by the time I'm thirty-five.
I do twenty-five reps per set.

PARENTHESES ( )

1. Enclose material that is not an essential part of the sentence, and that if not included would not alter its meaning:

In about three hours (two if we're lucky), the officers should pass out mail.
It was crazy (but justifiable) the way they stabbed that guy.

2. Often enclose letters or figures to indicate subdivisions of a series:

Please go online and do the following: (A) e-mail Michelle and let her know it's a go; (B) print me out the article about our new book; and (C) find out how much Photo Doctor will charge me to do the graphics for the cover of my new book.

NOTE: A closing parenthesis alone may be used in such lists: I need to a) get the medicine, b) give it to the dog, and c) step away quickly.

3. Enclose figures following and confirming written-out numbers in legal and business documents:

I will have it done in fifteen (15) days.
I will pay you one thousand dollars ($1,000.00) per original beat.

Note: This use is needed only in the most "Official" of documents – avoid it otherwise.

4. Enclose written-out words when the abbreviations are used for the first time and may be unfamiliar to the reader:

I am currently in Ad-Seg (Administrative Segregation).
I just came out of the SHU (Security Housing Unit).

NOTE: In court papers you'll do it the other way round, using the full term when first presented, followed by its acronym/abbreviation in parenthesis: I was placed into Administrative Segregation (AD-Seg)... After my hearing I was placed into a segregated housing unit (SHU). I wish the sourt tp know that Ad-Seg and the SHU are the same place, and treatment is no better as Ad-Seg.

PERIOD.

1. Terminates a complete declarative or mild imperative sentence:

I will write you tomorrow.
When you visit, bring money so we can eat.

2. Terminates outline indicators: 1., 2., XI., A., etc.

3. Serves as a decimal point: $4.50, 1.0" = 2.54 cm.

4. Serves to indicate subordination in a structured document: see explanation at I.V.A.3,C, where...

QUESTION MARK?

1. Terminates a direct question:

Are you going to pass out canteen tonight?

Is Nicki Minaj's ass bigger than Kim Kardashian's?

NOTE: A question mark is *not* used to terminate apparent questions caught up in plain text sentences: The captain asked if we were afraid of sharks.

QUOTATION MARKS (DOUBLE) " "

1. Enclose direct quotations:

In the beginning of the movie the officer said, "Ain't no talkin' when I'm talkin', fellas, so shut the fuck up."

2. Enclose words or phrases to clarify their meaning or use, or to indicate that they are being used in a special way:

"Playboy Business" represents a lifestyle.
I use the term "It's a new era" to express why I do what I do.
You got the "shit"?

QUOTATION MARKS (SINGLE)

1. Enclose quotations within quotations:

"In my opinion," he said, "the essence of the word 'beautiful' is Ninel Conde."
"Mike, your girl just called me and said, 'You better stop fuckin' with my man, bitch!' then hung up."

NOTE: Put commas and periods inside closing quotation marks; but put semicolons, colons, and dashes outside closing quotation marks. Other punctuation, such as exclamation points and question marks, should be put inside the closing quotation marks only if it is part of the matter quoted.

NOTE: "Go ahead, punk," he said, "make my day."
"Do you think you're lucky?"
Did he say, "I think I'm lucky?"

SEMICOLON ;

1. Separates the clauses of a compound sentence having no coordinating conjunction:

2. I'm the one who wrote the book; he's the one who typed it.

3. Chase money; once you catch it, everything you desire will chase you.

4. Separates elements of a series in which items already contain commas:

5. Within my inner circle, there's Playboy, the mack; Stranger Gonzales, the hitter; Sumo, the ladies' man; Cesar, the brute; and Johnny Boy, the young pit bull.

6. Separates clauses of a compound sentence joined by a conjunctive adverb, such as nonetheless, hence, or however:

7. Ol' girl's fine; however, she has a fucked-up attitude.

8. May be used instead of a comma to signal longer pauses for dramatic effect:

I'm about three things: money; power; and respect.

SLASH /

1. Means or "or" "and/or":

The drums and/or bassline are what made the beat pound so hard.

I'm looking for a Beyonce/Ciara/Rihanna type of girl.

NOTE: Avoid the slash generally, especially when it might easily be replaced with "and", make sure that the items joined with the slash are of the same class, not alternatives. Avoid "and/or" except in the rarest circumstances and/or when you wish to deliberately confuse your reader.

INMATE/URBAN WRITER'S RESOURCES

Here are a bunch of urban publishing companies, some of which will accept submissions. I've also included a bunch of companies that will help you get your book produced, some of which specialize in helping inmates. Keep in mind that a lot of these guys come and go, or re-locate, etc. To be safe, always send an inquiry letter and a SASE before sending them your work or any money.

4orPlay Publications, LLC
4100 Esters Rd. #286
Irving, TX 75038

This is an urban publishing company. They publish books like "East Boogie," "Silence is Secrecy," "4orPlay" and more.

They are now also accepting manuscripts for possible publishing. They want you to send the first 7 chapters, which are not to exceed 70 pages, and a synopsis.

Website:
4orPlayPublications.com

21st Street Urban Editing and Publishing
P.O Box 2033
Perris, CA 92572

This is an urban editing and publishing company, here are their submission guidelines: manuscript must be complete/ query letter/ synopsis/ submit first 5 chapters only – will request completed version if interested/ complete contact information including name, address, contact number, and email/ use 10 pt. font, double spaced, in manuscript-style format/ email all submissions/ allow up to 30 days for a response/ any manuscript not following these guidelines will be discarded immediately.

Website:
21streeturbanediting.com

A Million Thoughts Publishing
POB 872002
Mesquite, TX 75187

This company publishes/sells urban books, they ship **FREE** to prisoners. Write for a catalog.

APWA
198 College Hill Road
Clinton, NY 13323-1218

The American Prison Writing Archive Is an Internet-based, non-profit archive of first-hand testimony to the living and working conditions experienced by Incarcerated people, prison employees and prison volunteers.

Anyone who lives, works or volunteers Inside American prisons or jails can contribute non-fiction essays, based on first-hand experience: 5,000-word limit (15 double-spaced pages); a signed APWA permission-questionnaire must be Included In order to post on the APWA. All posted work will be accessible to anyone in the world with Internet access. For more Info and to download the permissions-questionnaire, go to www.dhinitiative.org/projects/apwa, or write to the address above.

The Beat Within

PO Box 34310
San Francisco, CA 94134

"We're a nonprofit organization that publishes the writing and artwork of incarcerated youth throughout the country. The Beat Withins' mission is to provide incarcerated youth with consistent opportunity to share their ideas and life experiences in a safe space that encourages literacy, self-expression, critical thinking skills, and healthy, supportive relationships with adults and their community. Outside of the juvenile justice system, The Beat Within partners with community organizations and individuals to bring resource to youth both inside and outside of detention. We are committed to being an effective bridge between youth who are locked up and the community that aims to support their progress towards a healthy, non-violent, and productive life.

The last few pages of our publication are dedicated to writing from incarcerated individuals outside of juvenile hall, which includes writing from jails, camps, ranches, prisons, etc., which is where your writing can be published.

We understand that in the past, subscriptions have been free. We regret to inform you that with such high demand, the cost of publication and postage, and the nature of our business (non-profit supported by a limited number of grants), we can no longer provide free subscriptions. Should you desire a specific copy or a subscription, please inquire and send a SASE. You can receive a **FREE** issue, however, if you are published. If published, we will send you the issue your writing appears in.

We look forward to reading your work and passing along your words to the youth and all Beat readers!"
EHU Publishing

The Cell Block

PO Box 1025
Rancho Cordova, CA 95741

The Cell Block is an independent multimedia company with the objective of accurately conveying the "street/prison" experience and

LIFE$TYLE, with the credibility and honesty that only one who has lived it can deliver, through literature and other arts, and to entertain and enlighten while doing so.

Available titles:

- The Best Resource Directory For Prisoners, by Mike Enemigo
- The Art & Power of Letter Writing for Prisoners, by Mike Enemigo
- Thee Enemy of the State, by Mike Enemigo
- Conspiracy Theory, by Mike Enemigo
- BASic Fundamentals of The Game, by Maurice "Mac BA$" Vasquez
- Loyalty & Betrayal, by Mike Enemigo & Armando Ibarra
- A Guide to Relapse Prevention for Prisoners, by Charles Hottinger Jr.
- Money IZ the Motive; By Mike Enemigo & Ca$ciou$ Green
- Money IZ the Motive 2; By Mike Enemigo & Ca$ciou$ Green
- Mob$tar Money; By Mike Enemigo & Ca$ciou$ Green
- Block Money; By Mike Enemigo & Ca$ciou$ Green
- Underworld Zilla, by Mike Enemigo & Guru
- How to Hustle & Win: Sex, Money, Murder; by Mike Enemigo & Guru
- This is my Life, by Crow

Website: thecellblock.net
Facebook: facebook.com/thecellblock.net
E-mail: thecellblock.net@mail.com

DC Book Diva Publications
#245 4401 – A Connecticut Ave, NW
Washington, DC 20008

This is an urban book publishing company that sells books for $15 plus $3.99 for S/H, but she will sell them to prisoners for $11.25 + $3.99 S/H.

Don Diva Magazine
603 W. 115th Street, #313
NY, NY 10025

Don Diva is an urban magazine – "the original street bible." A yearly subscription is $20.00; 4 issues a year. Single issues are $5.99 each. Send SASE for order form and info.

Website: dondivamag.com

Envisions Publishing
PO Box 451235
Houston, TX 77245

This is an urban book publishing company with a catalog that includes: Dark Horse Assassin, World War Gangster, MVP, MVP Reloaded, Wild Cherry, Preacherman Blues, Preacherman Blues 2, The Message, all by author Jihad; and Dynasty,

Dynasty 2, Dynasty 3, and Que, all by author Dutch. All books are $12.00 each. Buy 3, get a 4th **FREE**. Get a 15% discount on any of these books if you order from the website Jihadwrites.com.

Fast Lane Entertainment
#245 4401-A Connecticut Avenue, NW
Washington, DC 20008

This is the urban publishing company owned by national bestselling author Eyone Williams. Eyone is the official spokesman for the legendary DC thug Wayne Perry. Fast Lane offers titles 'Secrets Never Die,' 'Lorton Legends,' 'Money Ain't Everything', 'Never Lay Down' and more. Books are $15.00 with shipping.

Freebird Publishers
Box 541
North Dighton, MA 02764

They offer a bunch of services, products and publications. They "Service All Your Outside Needs With Inside Knowledge". Send SASE for more information.

Email: Diane@FreebirdPublishers.com,
Web: FreebirdPublishers.com

Gorilla Convict Publications
1019 Willott Rd.
St. Peters, MO 63376

Gorilla Convict is the publishing company operated and owned by incarcerated author Seth Ferranti. He's written such books as Prison Stories, Street Legends volume 1 and 2, and The Supreme Team, among others. His books are $15 each, plus $5.25 for s/h for the first book, and $2.25 for each additional book.

Comment: When I first decided books are what I'ma do I ordered two from Seth – Prison Stories and Street Legends (the first one). He wrote and published them from his prison cell so they inspired me and let me know it can be done. He's out now and runs the website gorillaconvict.com. I'll be sending him all my books this year in hopes of reviews. –Mike

Help From Beyond Walls
POB 185
Springvale, ME 04083

This is a prisoner services company that does it all: pen pals ads, stamp reimbursement, photo editing, gift ordering, internet reach, letter forwarding, website creation and much more. Write/Send SASE for more information.

Help From Outside
2620 Bellevue Way NE #200
Bellevue, WA 98004

Phone Number: 206-486-6042
Website: helpfromoutside.com

This company will help you accomplish the things you need to get done on the outside but can't – finance and business, social networking, phone calls, information, administrative work and more. Send SASE for a brochure and application.

Inmate Photo Provider
PO Box 2451
Forrest City, AR 72336

"Don't miss another special moment or event! Stay in the loop!

Have your FAMILY/FRIENDS text you UNLIMITED photos to (870) 317-7561 or email them to you at info@inmateprovider.com. All EMAIL/TEXT PHOTOS must include your full name, inmate number and address in the subject line in order for delivery to occur. If you ever go to the SHU, HOLE, or on LOCKDOWN at your facility, NO PROBLEM! We will continue to process your orders as long as funds are available in your prepaid account. Start your prepaid account today!) Minimum $10 deposit required.)

All photos are .50 cents per copy plus tax, shipping and handling. We also print social media photos from your Facebook page, Instagram account, Tagg, and the likes for .89 cents per copy, plus tax, shipping and handling! Our prices are based on the quality of service we provide. Photos are received and processed 24/7, seven days a week with quality service guaranteed for all local, state, federal and international inmates. Send your deposit to the above address today!

All deposits received will go toward processing your orders. For additional payment options, email us. Our representatives are standing by to assist you! We ACCEPT Money Orders, Institutional checks, JPay, MoneyGram (contact us for outside representative information to use this feature via email), family/friend debit or credit PayPal deposits are accepted. We do not accept personal checks. '

EXCLUSIVE FEATURE...

Add backgrounds, clothes and your loved ones to your photos! Starting at $15 (charges may vary according to your request and detail). Add $2.50 per additional photo used to create your photo. You must number your photo(s) and explain which features you want applied to your photo(s) on an additional sheet of paper. Based on your request, an additional 2-3 days may be needed to fulfill your order. For more information, see our Product & Service Description Pages in our catalog.

SOCIAL MEDIA...
SM Page Monitoring Packages available (prices vary). Email us at socialmedia@inmateprovider.com with questions.

NOW PROVIDING LOCAL NUMBERS ...

Affordable Inmate Calling Services, keeping you connected while saving you money! 100% Compliant! Make your everyday long-distance calls into local calls today! Receive (3) local numbers for only $22. With signing up today, earn (1) FREE MONTH of service ($10 activation fee included). You must provide us with the" first and last name of the contact personal for each line of service requested for verification and security purposes! Once payment is received, we will contact your family/friend to activate your account. We will email or mail you your local landline number after your account is set up.

Let IPP copy, Enlarge, and Collage your Photo(s) Today! 4x6, 5x7, 8x10 and wallet size services available, color or black and white!

To learn more about our magazine subscriptions, product, services, features and rates, simply write or email us at info@inmateprovider.com. To receive information from IPP, you must provide a SASE with your request, and if you are requesting our magazine listing, please send in (3) postage stamps

Comment: I received their catalog of photo manipulation examples. The quality looks pretty decent, especially for the price. They can take your head and put it on a body wearing a suit, or some other outfit that's better than your prison clothes. They can cut the background out of your prison photo and have you standing in front of a Bently, or in your city, whatever. – Mike

Internet Access Through Mail
4600 Monterey Oaks Blvd., #235
Austin, TX 78749

This company provides internet searches, as well as some email services. Write/Send SASE for more information.

King Poe Publishing
817 Bridle Drive
Desoto, TX 75115

Floyd "Poe" Simms is the author of 'How to Became a Millionaire Buying and Renting Properties in the Hood,' and 'Lil Poe: Drug Kingpin.' Each book is $15.99 plus $4.00 for s/h. You can order them direct.

LC DeVine Media, LLC
P.O. Box 4026
Flint, MI 48504

"Welcome! The Internet has changed how we do business and have created new avenues for business owners to bring the world to their place of business, searching for new ways to keep growing and earning profits. In the 21st Century a high percentage of people in the world have access to the Internet, businesses can virtually put their products and services online and have customers come to them from all over the world, instead of just their local communities. If you are a small store front, a progressive church, a company or a sole proprietor, let us help you do business 21st Century Style! That's doing business smarter, not harder! Some of the low cost, affordable services we include: Online advertising; unique website design; logo design; brochure design; business cards; post cards; signs; editing services; self-publishing; one-of-a-kind artworks.

Services/Prices: Typing, $1 per page; general editing, $2 per page (grammar and spelling clarity only); Copying, .15 for black and white, .30 for color (per page); Facebook page, $25 set-up only (you provide pic and info); Twitter page, $25 set-up only (you provide pic and info); Websites/Blogs, $200.00 set-up only (you provide pic and info); Website (3 pages), $350.00 set-up only (you supply picture and Info); E-book publishing, $500.00 complete set-up – copyright, ISBN, all profits yours; Printed book, $500.00 service fee, you pay all other expenses; E-book or printed paperback with company paying all costs, 50/50 contract deal. Fees are payable before work is done.

Please feel free to contact me if you desire any of the above services, or have any other services that I may assist you with. Sincerely, DeVine"LC Devine Media, LLC

Let My Fingers Do Your Typing
Sandra Z. Thomas
PO box 4178
Winter Park, FL 32793

This company provides typing services. Write/Send SASE for more information.

Manuscripts To Go
16420 Cooley Ranch Rd.
Geyderville, CA 95441

This company will help you with your manuscript(s). Write/Send SASE for more information.

The Marshall Project
156 West 56th St., Suite 701
New York, NY 10010

The background of The Marshall Project is that former New York Times Editor Bill Keller left the Times to start a new nonprofit news organization reporting solely on criminal justice, because he and many of the reporters now at The Marshall Project believed it was a pressing national issue that deserved an exclusive focus.

They launched in 2014, and the majority of their readers tend to be experts, advocates, practitioners, etc., with a direct interest in criminal justice. However, they do get a lot of readers from the general public, primarily because they co-publish many of their articles with publications like The Washington Post, The New York Times, Atlantic, Slate, Vice, etc.

ATTENTION ALL WRITERS!

Want your thoughts to be read in newspapers like The New York Times and The Washington Post? It can happen if you submit your writing to The Marshall Project. This is a call for submissions for The Marshall Project.

"The Marshall Project is a news organization that reports on the criminal justice system, including what happens inside jail and prisons. We have over 10,000 daily readers.

Part of what we do is publish first-person writing and reporting from inside jail and prisons, written by prisoners themselves. We want to give readers a sense of what life is like inside jails and prisons, and we believe that those who are actually inside are the best people to tell us.

If you are interested in writing for us – and reaching an audience of thousands of readers on the outside who want to know what life is like on the inside – here is some information about the type of writing we are looking for.

What we are looking for: Nonfiction writing about a specific aspect of life inside. Try to focus on one specific topic and tell a story about that topic. For example, tell us a story about a friendship you've made while inside; or a story about food or going to mess hall or commissary; or about how you get exercise; or about getting an education or having a job; or how you maintain relationships with family on the outside; or a story of your relationship with staff members; or the experience of solitary confinement or other forms of punishment.

The topic could be almost anything. The most important thing is to choose a very specific part of your experience and to write us a story about it.

What we are NOT looking for: Poetry, fiction, stories about your whole life (rather than a specific topic), essays about anything outside of your direct experience."

Length: 500-2,000 words

Please include your full name, how to contact you, and the url facebook.com/thecellblock.net

Midnight Express Books
PO Box 69
Berryville, AR 72616

"We've helped inmate author's self-publish books for over 10 years. We are the preferred service company helping inmate authors self-publish their work and the only company that publishes inmate's books full time. Helping inmate authors is all we do!

FREE standard ebook format included with every paid paperback book project!

2014 catalog of our authors' books available. To get your copy, send FIVE unused first class postage Forever stamps with your mailing address. Please print clearly.

Do you Corrlinks? We do! Sign up for our **FREE** monthly writing tips email programs. Only available via email; sorry.

Services/Prices...

Typing Services, starting at $3.50 per page: MEB is really excited to announce that we have put together a database of typists for our authors' use. Typing projects will be quoted individually and will be based on the quality of the handwriting and the documents themselves. That is to say that if the paper the project is written on is crumpled, torn or the handwriting is light, those projects will incur a higher rate. If you want you project quoted, please send in a complete copy along with any formatting requirements. We now also accept legal document typing and typing for documents other than manuscripts to be published.

Spanish Conversion, starting at $300.00: A new service we offer to authors we've already published. We'll take your book and cover and convert them to Spanish, assign them a new ISBN for a new paperback book and ebook. There are no proofs or drafts with this service.

Digital Covers, starting at $250.00: MEB will now provide access to our group of artists to prepare covers on book projects when we are not doing the entire book project. Prices will be more for just cover projects and will be quoted individually based on design concept submitted.

ISBN and Bar Codes; $200.00 with project, $250.00 without project: Authors who only need us to provide an independent ISBN registered to them or their company, with or without an entire project assignment.

Ebooks, starting at $200.00: For authors who have previously had a print bock prepared by a company other than MEB and who can provide the digital text file for the insides and pdf or indesign file for the cover, we will prepare an ebook for them and list it on Amazon for Kindle and Smashwords for distribution to other ebook retailers. Each project will be quoted independently."

Phone Number: 870-210-3772

Email: MEBooksl@yahoo.com

PEN American Center
588 Broadway, Suite 303
New York, NY 10012

The PEN's Prison Writing Program has three basic areas of concentration:

1. The Handbook For Writers In Prison. This handbook teaches elements of writing fiction, non-fiction, and poetry. It also provides resources for inmates in terms so next steps for their completed works. The Handbook is FREE for all prisoners who write us a letter requesting one.

2. Our annual Prison Writing Program awards contest. PEN awards cash prizes in five categories of writing from prisoners (fiction, essay, memoir, poetry, and drama/screenplay). We receive 1500 entries a year; the contest ends September 1st. We encourage inmates of all writing levels to enter the contest. To enter, simply mail the entry to the address above. No application or form is necessary, though most inmates do send us a short letter telling us a little bit about themselves. Winners lists are available upon request.

3. Our Mentor Program. The Prison Writing Mentorship Program pairs up established writer mentors with incarcerated mentees. Our program requires at least three exchanges of writing between mentees and mentors (that is, three submissions from mentees and three observations/commentaries to the submissions from mentors). To become eligible for the program, an inmate must first enter the annual contest. Winners are offered the opportunity to participate in the mentorship program and, in some instances, writers who do not win an award but show promise are also offered a mentor.

Prison Inmates Online
8033 W. Sunset Blvd. #7000
Los Angeles, CA 90046

"Prison Inmates Online is much more than a pen pal service. It's your link to the free world during your incarceration! A lot of inmates lose touch with family and friends after being incarcerated. With a PIO profile, friends and family can always find you, see what's going on in your life, and send you a message.

Keep your profile updated and never be forgotten. If you find love, don't pull your profile down, just change your relationship status to 'In a Relationship' in your bio and keep your profile going!"

Best value for your money: PIO is the best value for your online profile. Why pay more on other websites that only provide less? See how we compare to our competitors with better prices/service.

Profile price and renewals: PIO charges $50 for a profile that includes up to 300 words. Plus, every time you make a PAID update, your profile is extended for 1 year from the date of the update. Compare that to other websites who charge $40 for a profile that only contains 250 words and renewal rates up to $30 per year.

More photos than anyone else: PIO allows you to submit 5 photos with your profile. Compare that with the 1-2 photos most other services allow you to submit. Additional photos, art and tattoos are 5 for $10. Compare that to other websites that charge you $10 for EACH photo.

Featured Inmate: Our Featured Inmate panel is shown on nearly every page of PIO website and includes a courtesy in the 'ad' space section of the website. Compare that to other services who only show only show featured inmates on the homepage. Become a Featured Inmate for just $30 per month or $180 for the whole year!

Blogs and poems: List a blog or poem on PIO up to 300 words for just $10. Compare that to the $15 other websites charge. Other services like videos, tattoos and documents aren't even provided by other websites.

Documents section: Share documents (legal, stories, journals, diaries) for others to view or download. A great way to inform people who are following you or your case! It's also a rest place to store digital copies of your records in one place. Only $10 for each document title, up to 50 pages.

Tattoo section: Many men and women are drawn to people with tattoos. Why not show off yours in the tattoo section? The photos of your tattoos are linked to your profile page so it's another way to get more visitors to your page. $10 for up to 5 photos.

Videos: YouTube is the Internet's largest video sharing website and is integrated into this site. You can post any video that is listed on YouTube directly to your profile page. Your favorite music video, comedian, or even your own videos if they are posted on YouTube! Only $5 per video!"

Website: prisoninmates.com
Corrlinks: infoprisoninmates.com

Comment: This may very well be the best profile service I've seen. You can practically have everything a real, personal/company website can have. – Mike

Prisons Foundation
2512 Virginia Ave. NW #58043
Washington, DC 20037

They will publish any book written by a prisoner, as is on their website. Send a SASE for complete guidelines.

Supreme Design
PO Box 10887
Atlanta, GA 30310

Supreme Design is a publishing company operated by Supreme Understanding. Supreme Understanding is a community activist, educator, and expert on the socioeconomically and psychological struggles of oppressed people. His extensive research and life experience helped him design a system of success for even the most disadvantaged. The following books are available...

• How to Hustle and Win, Part 1: A Survival Guide for the Ghetto, by Supreme Understanding (Forward by the Real Rick Ross)

This is the book that started it all. Now an international bestseller, this book has revolutionized the way people think of "urban literature." It offers a street-based analysis of social problems, plus practical solutions that anyone can put to use. 336 pages, $14.90 (ISBN: 978-9816170-0-8)

• How to Hustle and Win, Part 2: Rap, Race, and Revolution; by Supreme Understanding (Forward by Sticamn of Dead Prez)

The controversial follow up to How to Hustle and Win digs even deeper into the problems we face, and how we can solve them. Part 1 focused on personal change, and Part 2 explores the biggest picture of changing the entire hood. 384 pages, $14.95 (ISBN: 978-9816170-9-1)

• La Brega: Como Sobrevivir En El Barrio, by Supreme Understanding

Thanks to a strong demand from Spanish-speaking countries, we translated our groundbreaking "How to Hustle and Win" into Spanish, and added new content specific to Latin America. Because this book's language is easy to follow, it can also be used to brush up on your Spanish. 336 pages, $14.95 (ISBN: 978-0981617-08-4)

- Locked Up But Not Locked Down: A Guide to Surviving the American Prison System, by Ahmariah Jackson and IAtomic Allah (Forward by Mumia Abu Jamal)

This book covers what it's like on the inside, how to make the most out of your time, what to do once you're out, and how to stay out. Features contributions from over 50 insiders, covering city jails, state and federal prisons, women's prisons, juvenile detention, and international prisons. 288 pages, $14.95 (ISBN: 978-1935721-00-0)

- Knowledge of Self: A Collection of Wisdom on the Science of Everything in Life; edited by Supreme Understanding, C'BS Alife Allah, and Sunez Allah (Forward by Lord Jamar of Brand Nubian)

Who are the Five Percent? Why are they here? In this book, over 50 Five Percenters from around the world speak for themselves, providing a comprehensive introduction to the esoteric teaching of the Nation of Gods and Earths. 256 pages, $14.95 (ISBN: 978-1935721-67-3)

- The Science of Self: Man, God, and the Mathematical Language of Nature, by Supreme Understanding and C'BS Alife Allah (Forward by Dick Gregory)

How did the universe begin? Is there a pattern to everything that happens? What's the meaning of life? What does science tell us about the depths of our SELF? Who and what is God? This may be one of the deepest books you can read. 360 pages, $19.95 (ISBN: 978-1935721-67-3)

- The Hood Health Handbook, Volume 1 (Physical Health). Ed. by Supreme Understanding and C'BS Alife Allah (Forward by Dick Gregory)

Want to know why Black and Brown people are so sick? This book cover the many "unnatural causes" behind poor health, and offers hundreds of affordable and easy-to-implement solutions. 480 pages, $19.95 (ISBN: 978-1-936721-32-1)

- The Hood Health Handbook, Volume 2 (Mental Health), Ed. by Supreme Understanding and C'BS Alife Allah

This volume covers mental health, how to keep a healthy home, raising healthy children, environmental issues, and dozens of other issues, all from the same down-to-earth perspective as Volume 1. 480 pages, $19.95 (ISBN: 978-1-935721-33-8)

SureShot Books Publishing LLC
PO Box 924
Nyack, NY 10960
Attn: Publishing Dept.

SureShot Books works with authors every day to have their work published in a professional and timely manner. SureShot Books Publishing LLC packages start at $895 and can fluctuate depending on your manuscript. At SureShot Books Publishing LLC, the author receives 100 percent of their royalties and will also own the rights to their work. All accepted books will appear in our catalog and on our website.

To submit your work for consideration, submissions should follow this format:

- First three chapters only
- One paragraph synopsis of each of the three chapters
- One-page synopsis of entire book
- One paragraph of what you'd say on the back of your book

Books that are not formatted in the manner outlined will be rejected. After our team has reviewed your work, we may request further chapters or the entire novel. Please allow four-six weeks for a response.

We look forward to being your next publishing platform.

For over 1,400 up-to-date resources of non-nude photo companies, book sellers, legal help, and much, much more, order *The BEST Resource Directory For Prisoners.* NOW, for only $19.99 + $7 s/h. No order form needed, just write clearly on a piece of paper and send payment to The Cell Block!

DEVILS & DEMONS

Yada was sitting low in the driver's seat of his car. It was parked next to a trash bin in the back of the parking lot, across from room 112. Yada was waiting for Alize to show up with the weed Nirobi – Yada's cousin and crime partner – was gonna "buy," so he could follow her back to her place of residence and jack the bitch. As he sat there alone, he thought about how he would take his Buick straight to the paint shop after robbing Ze for everything she had. He was tired of riding around in a bucket with its back window busted out. He couldn't even open his trunk without the help of a screwdriver. Now that he had money, it was time to upgrade.

He was in the process of fantasizing about trips to Miami when he saw the burgundy Malibu pull into the parking space directly in front of room 112. A white girl with red hair and a fat ass stepped out of the driver's side. *That's gotta be Ze right there*, Yada thought to himself. He knew she was a stripper, and he could see why a nigga would throw money at that. Then the passenger side opened and another female got out. This one was shorter, but just as sexy. She was wearing a white button-up and a pair of capris. They both had on stilettoes and large sunglasses. They weren't the normal tennis-shoe-wearing females that he was used to dealing with. This intrigued him, so he decided to take a closer look, and after Nirobi opened the door and let them inside, Yada switched the game plan.

When the girls stepped inside the motel room, they were welcomed by the aroma of expensive weed and liquor. It was obvious that Nirobi had rented the room to party. That was cool with the girls; free weed and drinks were always welcome.

Nirobi led them to the couch. After they sat down, he said, "Man, Ze, I didn't know you was bringing a friend."

"This is my sister, Brittany. Brit-Brit, this is Nirobi." Brittany purposely blushed, making herself look innocently cute.

"I brought the trees," began Ze, "but it's in the car."

"That's cool, I got the money right—"

Nirobi was cut off in mid-sentence when the door suddenly opened and a light-skinned man wearing a diamond O.P. pendant that looked exactly like Talton's stepped inside. For those of you who don't know, Talton is a known gangsta from Oak Park, a grimy neighborhood in Sacramento, California, ran by Underworld Zilla Bloods.

Alize shot up out of her seat, "What the hell is this?"

"It's good," said Nirobi. "This is my cousin, Yada. He's cool." Nirobi was surprised at the sudden change of plans. He wasn't sure what would happen next, but he hoped Yada had decided to hang out with the females before they did anything; he was dying for a chance to mess around with Alize.

Ze didn't like surprises, but her sister did. Brittany stood up, extending her hand towards the light-skinned intruder. "How you doing, Mr.Yada? I'm Brit-Brit, and this is my sister, Alize."

Yada took Brittany's hand and said, "Nice to meet you Brit-Brit." Then he turned to look at Alize; "My bad if I caught you off guard. I was just—"

"I knew you were out there. You were sitting in the scraper next to the trash bin."

Damn, she's sharp, thought Yada. "Yeah, I was rollin' a blunt. When I saw you show up I came in to introduce myself. My cousin tells me you got pounds, but he didn't tell me you had a friend."

"She's my sister," said Ze.

"Shit... that's what's up," continued Yada. "Go ahead, get settled in. Let your hair down, have a few drinks, let's smoke some trees."

Alize did a quick inventory of the situation. Brittany was giving her a look of approval; it seemed like everything was on the up and up. She really didn't have anywhere else to be, and it had been a long time since she and her sister had partied together, so why not? *You only live once*, she told herself. "You know what... I can use a drink. And somebody needs to put on some music."

After that, it was on. Nirobi put on a J. Cole CD, and before long, everyone was tipsy. Alize found the thermometer and turned up the heat. In no time, the guys were in their boxers and the sisters were almost naked. Brittany was wearing a pink bra with matching boy shorts. Alize had on lace; Victoria's Secret. Smoke was in the air, drinks were spilling and the mood was festive.

It wasn't long before Brittany and Yada went to the bathroom to take a shower together. That's when Alize found herself alone with Nirobi. She hadn't had sex in months and couldn't think of a reason why a little casual sex shouldn't happen. Nirobi wasn't bad looking. In the back of her mind, she had always wondered what it would be like being with him, so she went for it.

Somewhere in the background, she heard a phone vibrating. From the sound of its location, she could tell that it was her phone. Nevertheless, she ignored it, choosing sex with Nirobi over business.

Nirobi was sitting on the couch watching Ze dance. Earlier they had moved the coffee table, so nothing was blocking her from seductively gyrating towards the young thug. He was memorized by the way she ran her fingers through her hair and manipulated her hips.

Alize worked her way towards Nirobi, eventually kneeling down in front of him; all the while, keeping constant eye contact with him as she took his boxers off. She then spread his legs and looked at his penis. That's when she found herself face-to-face with the smallest dick she had ever seen on a grown man. It was maybe two inches long, and as thick as her pinky. If she had had any goals of getting her cat beat up, they were crushed at the sight of his childlike manhood.

A part of her wanted to get up right then and there, but that would've been cruel. Instead, she took his penis between her thumb and index finger, holding it up while she put her lips on it. Alize had enough experience with different-sized men, but this was comical. His manhood wouldn't even reach to the back of her throat. Instead of deep throating it, the only thing she could do was massage it with her tongue. She would've broke out laughing if it weren't so sad, so she did her best with what he had.

Luckily her mate was a premature ejaculator; she was saved by his lack of sexual control. The moment she tasted his cum in her mouth she quickly climbed his body and kissed him on the mouth, transferring his own fluids from her mouth into his. She would've never done that to a man she respected, but this was turning out to be a joke.

As they were kissing, Alize positioned herself beneath Nirobi. Then she pushed him down until his body was off the couch and his face was in between her legs. She then took off her panties and bra and leaned back as far as she could, putting the bottom of her feet on the edge of the couch. After that she spread her thighs so that her wet pussy was in Nirobi's face.

Alize had thick pussy lips. So thick that they had to be physically parted in order for someone to see the entrance to her vagina. Before Nirobi spread open her lower lips he saw her swollen clitoris sticking out like a tiny penis. And, once he did open them, he couldn't believe how small her pussy was.

Ze's sex cave was wet with eagerness. Nirobi was so close he could see the liquids slowly oozing out of it. He took two fingers and saturated them in her juices, then stuck them inside of her. The sudden penetration forced Alize to pull back, but not for long. Within seconds, she began rocking her hips to the rhythm of his foreplay. Then Nirobi put his mouth on her clit and started massaging it with his tongue like she had done to him only moments earlier.

In the background, Ze heard pounding coming from the bathroom. Her sister was yelling like Yada's dick was killing her. She would've been jealous if it weren't for the fact that Nirobi's tongue play was above average. He sucked her clit at the same time as he tickled her G-spot with the tips of his fingers.

With his fingers inside of her, Alize started rocking her body faster and faster. It felt surprisingly invigorating; so much so that she soon felt an orgasm mounting. All the while, her sister was moaning loudly in the background. And, could that have been her phone vibrating again? She didn't care... she was about to cum!

All she wanted to do was reach that summit. "Keep going, Nirobi! Don't stop, God damn it!" She couldn't hold it any longer; she needed a penis no matter how small it was. Ze grabbed Nirobi roughly, pulling him on top of her, sliding his diminutive phallus into her tight subway. All in one motion she reached around his back and slid her middle and index fingers into his rectum. It all happened so fast, Nirobi didn't have a chance to react. Alize then used her tight grip to control his body, pushing and pulling him in and out of her as fast and as hard as she possibly could; the whole time, digging her fingers into his anus maliciously.

"Don't stop!" yelled Ze as she pulled him against her body. "Don't fucking stop!"

Nirobi couldn't have stopped if he wanted to. Alize had her eyes shut while she masturbated with his body. Then, suddenly she began shaking uncontrollably. She had finally reached the peak she had longed for. Wave after wave of ecstasy shot through her loins, shocking her senses. She didn't want the moment to end. She kept her fingers inside of him as if daring him to stop, not letting him go until she had sucked every ounce of erotic energy from his soul.

A few seconds went by, then she heard her phone again. She also realized that the moaning in the bathroom had stopped. Her pussy felt good, but she had to snap back to reality. It wasn't the painful, dominating sex that she wanted from Talton, yet it was pleasing. Nirobi had been better than her fingers in the shower.

Alize disengaged herself from Nirobi, then gave him a little push, causing him to roll onto the spot next to her. Seeing the shocked expression on his face made her laugh out loud.

"What's wrong with you?" she asked. "It looks like you just got violated." Alize smiled as she stood up. Still naked, she walked towards the table where her phone was at. After picking it up she headed toward the bathroom. She didn't knock on the door; she was deliberately trying to catch a glimpse at the piece of flesh that made her sister scream so loud. But when she stepped in, all she found was Brittany kissing a towel-clad Yada. "Girl, I gotta pee," said Ze as she walked around them.

Yada snickered when Alize sat on the toilet. Then he said, "I guess I'll give y'all some girl time." After giving Brittany one last kiss, he left the room.

As soon as the door shut behind him, the girls looked at one another and started giggling.

"Damn, bitch!" said Ze. "It sounded like he was killing you!"

"He's a beast, sis! Oh, my God... it was so big it was *ugly*. And he wouldn't stop. He just kept ramming that thing up in me! God, that dick was good. What about yours? You look like you just busted a *good* one."

"I'll tell you later."

"Tell me what?"

Alize had started checking her text messages. The first one read: Attached is a video from last night. If you recognize this guy, GET AT ME ASAP!!!

Ze activated the video link and gasped when she realized what she was watching.

"What's wrong?" asked Brittany.

"It's a video of my friend's brother getting killed."

"For real? Move, let me see!" Brittany leaned in and watched for several seconds before saying, "Oh fuck! Ze, that's Yada!"

Suddenly on alert, Alize said, "I know. Listen, go out there and get our clothes. Don't act suspicious, just get our stuff. Hurry up!"

"What're you gonna do?"

"Just get our stuff, we're leaving."

$$$$$

Talton was devastated. Last night, his brother, Anthony, was killed by a sucka who robbed him of his cash and jewels, including the O.P. medallion that hung from his neck; the only one in the world that exists besides Talton's own. Luckily, Ant was face-timing with his wife, Angelique, who pressed record when the scuffle began, catching a glimpse of the murderer. Talton didn't recognize the man, but at least he had a face to hunt. In a desperate measure to find his brother's killer, he e-mailed the video to all of his street connects to see if anyone recognized him.

Talton was driving aimlessly in a G-ride, plotting on his next move when he felt his phone vibrate. When he glanced at it, he saw it was Alize tappin' in, so he decided to answer.

"What's good? Did you get my text?"

"Yeah," replied Ze, "but, listen. Can you get to the Days Inn on U.S. 19?"

"Yeah, but what for?"

"The guy on that video is here right now! I'm in his bathroom."

"Are you absolutely sure it's him?" asked Talton, suddenly feeling as if he was just injected with a shot of pure adrenaline. Before Ze had the chance to reply, he was already in the process of making a reckless U-turn in the middle of oncoming traffic.

"I'm a thousand percent positive it's him," she whispered. "He's even wearing a medallion like yours."

Talton's vision became blurred at the mention of his brother's necklace. He had to fight to hold the tears from falling. "What room are y'all in?"

"112; first floor, towards the back. But, you gotta hurry. I'm leaving right now."

$$$$$

Alize had just ended the call when the bathroom door opened and in came Yada. She had no idea whether he had heard her conversation with Talton, and it must have shown on her face because Yada said, "What's wrong with you? My little cousin must've blown your mind out there. He's looking just like you – like he just lost his virginity, or something."

Yada squatted down to pick up his things from the bathroom floor. When he did, Alize saw a pistol. Nevertheless, she slid a seductive smile on her face and said, "Lost his virginity, huh? Well, maybe he did. You wanna smell my finger?"

Ze stood up, still naked, and started washing her hands in the sink. That's when Brittany came in with their clothes. Yada stepped out the way so she could pass by. She went to the toilet, closed the lid, and sat down to put her clothes on.

Yada was still wrapped in his towel. As he stood there staring at Ze's plump backside, the sight of it was beginning to overwhelm him. It was obvious what was happening and the sisters watched as he slowly started to grow underneath the towel. From the long rising bulge, Alize could clearly see that he was working with over a foot of massive piping.

"Damn, sis!" exclaimed Ze. "I see why you sounded as if he was rippin' you apart!"

"I told you he was a beast."

"Oh, yeah, I'ma beast alright." Yada undid the knot in the towel, letting it fall to the floor. Without anything suppressing it, Yada's humongous member hopped around uncontrollably, twitching like it had a mind of its own, oozing with precum as if it were salivating at the prospect of more pussy. "If you want, we can make this a family affair."

Ze stared at the huge penis in front of her, then turned and looked at her sister. After a few seconds, they both started giggling. Turning back to Yada, she reached out and grabbed the head of his hammer. Holding it like it was a doorknob, she gave it a light squeeze before saying, "I'll have to take a rain check on this one. But, I'll definitely be calling real soon."

Yada's member fought against her grip, surprising Alize with its power. It was like an animal, spoiling for a fight.

Yada had never been turned on so much in his life. He felt like he could cum right there, on the middle of the floor. Yet, that would be a major embarrassment, showing that he had no sexual control, so he decided to leave the room before he had an accident. "Alright, then. I'ma give y'all some privacy." He quickly backed out of the bathroom, clothes in hand.

"You do that," said Ze. "We'll be out there in a minute." After shutting the door behind him she turned to her sister.

"Hurry up, bitch! Get dressed! There's gonna be bullets flying all over the place!"

"What'd you do?"

"Don't worry about it. Just get dressed. We gotta get outta here."

They both raced to put their clothes on. Alize was in so much of a hurry, she forgot to put her panties on, stuffing them in her pocket, instead.

In the main room, Yada was getting dressed, too, making sure to leave his newly acquired necklace visible. Nirobi still hadn't said a word, but that didn't bother the older cousin. He was on top of the world, feeling like he just hit the lottery, totally blind to the fact that by the end of the night, one of them would be dead, and the other would be handcuffed to a hospital bed...

$$\$\$\$\$\$$

Talton was speeding through busy traffic, already having narrowly missed several accidents. His body felt warm as the adrenaline raced through his veins. Reaching under his seat, he found his chrome Desert Eagle and placed it on his lap. He didn't have to make sure it was loaded because he kept it filled with hollow heads.

The objective was simple: Catch up with his brother's killer and murder him.

$$\$\$\$\$\$$

Alize and Brittany both came out of the restroom fully dressed. Nirobi was putting his pants on and Yada was sitting at the table, tying his shoe laces. The girls wanted to leave before the shooting started, but their suitors had different plans.

"Why y'all looking like you 'bout to run out on us?" asked Yada from the far end of the room.

"We gotta go," said Ze. "Nirobi, I just got another call, so I'ma go get your weed out the trunk."

"But we still got more drank. You ain't gotta go so soon, do you?" Nirobi asked, pleadingly.

Alize's phone sounded again. "See, that's them right now." She looked at her phone and read the text from Talton: STALL EM! Ze stared at the message for a moment, thinking of the possible ramifications of prolonging her involvement in what was about to happen. She knew she should leave; she had done enough. Yet, something more innate told her to stay. So when she looked up from her phone, what she said next surprised everyone. "Forget that other sale. We can hang out a lil longer."

"That's what I'm talking 'bout!" called out Yada from across the room.

Brittany didn't seem to agree with her sister's sudden change of plans. "Ze, I think we better go. We can meet up with these guys later. At least let's go get this money, then come back."

"I got money right here," said Nirobi from his spot on the couch. "A bird in the hand is better than two in the bush, right, Ze?"

"You damn right, baby. Go ahead and roll another blunt." With that, she walked over to the couch and sat down next to Nirobi.

Brittany stood in the middle of the room trying to make eye contact with her sister, but Ze wouldn't look at her. It was obvious that her sister was stalling for some reason, but she couldn't understand why. This had nothing to do with them; they needed to get out before things got too hot. It wasn't that she was afraid. On the contrary, Brittany was good under fire, but this wasn't making any sense. They hadn't been involved in anything like this since their teenage years, and now, Alize was forcing them to jump in head first.

"Brit-Brit, come sit wit' your boy," said Yada. "Why you over there looking lost?"

She tried to smile. "Hold on, I gotta use the bathroom. You put a hurtin' on this pussy. I don't know what's up with me." Brittany went back in the restroom with a sudden urge to urinate. On her way, she gave her sister one last glance, but Alize refused to look up.

$$$$$

Talton turned into the Days Inn, quickly slowing down so as not to attract any unnecessary attention.

He knew exactly where to go. He'd been there on several occasions. The Days Inn was built like an apartment complex, with the driveway going all the way around its square layout. All the doors to the rooms faced the driveway. There was also a courtyard with a pool in the center, which was only visible from the rooms. Surrounding the motel was a wooden fence that separated it from a residential area.

Talton found Alize's car parked in front of room 112. After stopping the truck, he cocked his cannon and prepared to leave the vehicle.

$$$$$

Alize had just taken a hit from the blunt when Brittany came out of the bathroom. When they looked at one another, Brittany shot her a glance that said, "Let's go!", and Ze replied with a look that said, "Give me a sec."

Then, their wordless conversation was cut short by Alize's phone. It was another text from Talton; this time it read: "Get out, NOW!!!" It was all the prompting she needed. Alize hopped out of her seat, loudly announcing,

"Well... it's time for us to go, guys. I'ma go get your weed, Nirobi—"

Before she could finish her statement, a deep banging sound came from the door to the room. It sounded like someone was trying to kick it open. Suddenly, the door snapped off its hinges and came crashing onto the floor. Everyone was caught off guard, giving Talton the edge he needed. It took a second for Yada, the sole person in the room with a gun, to assess the threat and reach for his weapon. Still, he was too slow.

As if his brother's O.P. medallion was a hone-in device, Talton zeroed in on it immediately. Ignoring everyone else in the room, he entered in with his cannon in shooting position and quickly let off four deafening rounds, all of them aimed straight into his target's face. Upon impact, the bullets exploded, causing blood and brain matter to be grossly discarded in all directions, but mostly against the sliding glass door where Yada's lifeless body had fallen.

Everything in Talton's mind was moving in slow motion. Alize ran towards her sister and they both sprinted towards the door. That's when Talton saw the dread sitting on the couch. This had to be the "Nirobi" character you could hear the other one calling, on the video, after killing Ant. Therefore, in Talton's eyes, he was an accomplice.

Talton slowly lifted his Desert Eagle, wanting to savor the moment. When Nirobi realized what was happening, he dived off the couch, but it was too late. Boom! Boom! Boom! Fire shot out of the tip of the gun every time Talton pulled his finger. Nirobi's torso flipped sideways as the bullets destroyed his upper chest cavity.

Talton heard Alize trying to get his attention, but his mind didn't register what she was saying. He needed Ant's necklace; it was a piece of his brother and he had to have it. With only one thing on his mind, Talton lowered his gun and walked towards his first victim.

The near-headless body lay slumped against the glass door, still spitting blood from its main artery. The man's heart must have missed the memo. It was over; there was no way he was coming back from that. Talton walked up to the dead body, reached down and snatched Anthony's bloody necklace from the marauder's neck. He then put it on, letting it rest next to its twin.

That's when the world around Talton began to speed up. Now he could hear and understand what Alize was trying to tell him. From the doorway, she was yelling, "Hurry up! Come on, Talton!" Then, in the background, he heard a man's voice, "Call the police!" That woke Talton all the way up.

Alize and Brit jumped in the driver's seat, Ze the passenger's. Talton followed, but he stopped just short of the door. As the Malibu was backing out, Ze called for Talton to get in, but he ignored her. Instead, he took off running towards the back of the complex. After hopping the gate and a few more fences after that, Talton found himself walking down a quiet street in the heart of someone's neighborhood. He then took off his black and red True Religion T-shirt and wrapped it around his head. He also took off both necklaces, putting them in his jean pocket.

Within minutes he emerged from the subdivision. Finding a Seven Eleven on the other side of a busy intersection, Talton headed straight for it. He knew from experience that it was better to hide in plain sight.

Brittany had driven away from the room in a rush. Alize was upset with Talton for not getting in the car, yet, deep down, she knew that he had made the right decision by running the other way. At the entrance of the Days Inn, the girls should've taken a left to head home. Instead, Alize told Brittany to go east and circle the area in search for Talton. After hitting a few corners they saw a man in a white tank top walking towards the Seven Eleven. It was him, so Brittany pulled into the convenient store's parking lot.

When she stopped, Alize convinced Talton to get in. Seconds later they were safely driving away, undetected by the law...

When Talton leaves the West Coast to set up shop in Florida, he meets the female version of himself: A drug-dealing murderess with psychological issues. A whirlwind of sex, money and murder inevitable ensues and Talton finds himself on the run from the law with nowhere to turn to. When his team from home finds out he's in trouble, they get on a plane heading south....

Devils & Demons, by Mike Enemigo, Dutch & King Guru, available now on thecellblock.net and Amazon, or by sending $15 plus $5 S/H to The Cell Block; POB 1025; Rancho Cordova, CA 95741

CONSPIRACY THEORY

October 5, 1998

It's about 75-100 Gs worth of weed and it'll
be easy as fuck. -- Kevin

I was at home asleep on my futon when the phone rang.

"Hello," I said drowsily.

"What up, man? Kevin." Kevin is my cousin. Our fathers are twins.

"Oh, what's up?"

"What're you doin' right now?"

"Shit, I was knocked out," I said.

"Oh, OK. Well, you want me to call you back?"

"Yeah, give me about 15 minutes, then hit me back up."

"OK. I'll be back at you in 15."

I laid back down on my futon and closed my eyes while trying my best to shake off the sleepiness. Fifteen to twenty minutes quickly passed and the phone rang again.

"What up?" I asked a bit more alive than I had the first time around.

"What's up, man, you up?"

"Yeah, I'm up. What's going on?"

"Well, I'm calling because I got a lick, and I wanna know if you're interested."

"What kind of lick?" I asked.

199

"It's about 75-100 Gs worth of weed, and it'll be easy as fuck."

"Oh yeah? Where's it at?"

"It's in a backyard, somewhere in Fair Oaks. I'm not sure exactly, I gotta talk to Bryan. But they got Christmas tree-size plants, a bunch of 'em, and all you gotta do is hop over the fence, cut 'em down, and be out. Plus, right now, nobody's home," he added.

"Nobody's home?"

"Naw, they're at the hospital."

"For what?"

"Well, earlier today a couple of guys I know tried to get the plants. They kicked the door in and ran up in there, and they ended up beating the guy's son with a baseball bat or something. They made off with 1-2 plants but that's it; the rest is still there and the family is at the hospital with the son."

"OK. So all I gotta do is hop the fence, cut down the plants, and leave?" I asked semi-curious. It sounded like a pretty easy job.

"That's it. But you're gonna need 1-2 more people. You won't be able to do it all yourself. You're gonna need trash bags and some kind of hacksaw or something, too. It's a ton of weed. Bomb."

"OK, well, you ain't got nobody else?" I asked.

"Naw, I tried a couple of guys but they don't wanna do it. So now I'm hittin' you up. You interested?"

"Um…I guess I could holla at my boy and see if he wants to fuck with it. Let me hit him up and I'll call you back in 30 minutes, maybe an hour. Is that cool?"

"Yeah, that's cool. Hit me back."

After we hung up I called my friend Loki, but he didn't answer. He was like that sometimes, where he wouldn't answer the phone even if he was home, so I decided to get in my 1970 Cougar and drive to his apartment, which was just a couple miles down the street.

When I got to Loki's apartment I noticed his car was not parked in its usual spot. However, he and his girlfriend only had one car at the time, so just in case he was inside, I went up and knocked on his door.

No answer.

Well, I guess that's that. I scribbled a note, stuck it on his door, then got in my car and went back home.

When I arrived at my apartment, I called Kevin back.

"Hello," he said as he picked up the phone.

"It's me," I said.

"What's the verdict?"

"Naw, it's all bad. I went by my boy's house but he wasn't home. I left a note on his door to hit me up ASAP or to meet me at the studio. I ain't really got nobody else. If I find someone, though, I'll send 'em your way."

"All right. Let me know."

"A'ight, fa sho," I said as I hung up the phone.

I got up and started to gather the things I needed for my studio session which was scheduled for 10:00 PM. I was putting together a hip-hop CD and I needed to dump some of the beats I had from my ASR-X Pro onto DATs (digital audio tapes). I had recently started using two studios; Hitworks on Auburn Boulevard and Champion Sounds on Fruitridge. Hitworks was a little less expensive, so I used all the time I had there to dump all my beats and things. Then I'd record my vocals and get my mixes at Champion Sounds. Tonight I had to dump some beats so I was off to Hitworks.

The phone rang again.

"Hello?"

"Hey, babe, what's up?" It was my girlfriend, Nicki.

"Shit, about to go to the studio. What's crackin'?"

"Well, I'm glad I caught you before you left. Anyway, Ruben" – Ruben is her son – "wants to stay at my mom's house tonight. Can you put some of his clothes, a pair of shoes, and a couple of his toys in his backpack and drop it off at her house?"

"Yeah, I can do that. And since we're talking, go on and make me something to eat. After I drop the stuff off at your mom's, I'll swing by and pick up the food on my way to the studio."

"OK, no problem. Chicken strips and fries?" she asked.

"Yeah."

"All right. I'll have it ready. See you soon, OK?"

"See you soon. Oh, call Jimmy and tell him to meet me out front."

"OK. I love you."

"I love you too," I echoed before hanging up.

I went around the apartment and gathered the things I'd been asked to take over for Ruben. Then, after double checking to make sure I had everything I needed for both the studio session and Ruben's sleepover, I got into my car and drove a couple of neighborhoods over to Becky's house.

Becky is my girlfriend's mom, Ruben's grandmother. Becky and I were never on the best of terms – which I'll explain a bit more to you later – but we did our best to remain polite with one another. Well, at least in front of each other. I'm certain I was the subject of many of Becky's complaints when I wasn't around. Nevertheless, I wanted to fit in with my girlfriend's family and get along with her mother, so I tried to help out and be as cooperative as I could. Despite this, however, I wanted to avoid awkward dealings as much as possible, which is why I had my girlfriend tell her youngest brother, Jimmy, who out of her family liked me more than anybody else, meet me out front of Becky's house.

$$$$$

As I pulled up to Becky's house about 10 minutes later I saw Jimmy, waiting patiently.

"What's up, Jimmy?"

"What's up, what's going on?" he asked.

"Oh, you know, 'bout to go to the studio. Just droppin' off Ruben's backpack first. I guess he's gonna stay with you guys tonight, huh?"

"Yeah, Nicki's working pretty late tonight anyway, so instead of waking him up to take him home, he'll just stay here."

"Yeah, that's cool. Well, here's his backpack, OK? I gotta get going. I'm gonna stop by your sister's job and get some food before heading off to the studio."

"OK. Take care of yourself," he said.

"You too," I replied before driving off.

Jimmy's a cool kid. I did my best to mentor him a little bit – encourage him to stay out of trouble and stuff like that. Shit, at this time he must've been about 12 years old. Even though he has two older brothers, they didn't seem to pay him much attention or offer much guidance, and since he took a liking to me, I'd let him come around from time to time.

I arrived at my girlfriend's job, which was Lyon's restaurant, where she was a manager at, about 3 minutes after leaving Becky's house. When I got there I saw her brother David, who also worked at Lyon's, as a cook, out front smoking a cigarette...

I first met David (and his brother Dennis) in 1994 at a mutual friend's house; sometime in the first or second month, if my calculations are correct. We were both 14 years old at the time and we clicked instantly.

The same day I met David is when I met the rest of his immediate family, a little later, when they came over to our mutual friend's house to pick him and Dennis up. It was Becky, his mother; Charles, his stepfather; Jimmy, his youngest brother; Darlene, his older sister; and Nicki, who was pregnant at the time, the oldest of all the siblings at 18, and now, of course, my girlfriend.

I remember thinking that David's family was pretty cool. Theirs was much different than mine; they were originally from East L.A. and had that whole East L.A. gangster style I thought was cool at the time. Shit, even Becky was an ex-chola who went by the nickname of Payasa. Being from Sac I had a different get-down, but respected theirs – something I'd only experienced before by watching movies, as I'd never been anywhere near East L.A.

Me and David quickly became best friends. We were inseparable. Either he'd be at my house where I lived with my father and stepmother, or I'd be at his. Usually I'd be at his, though, because while my dad is cool as hell, he had very little understanding of or experience with the lifestyle I thought was attractive as an adolescent, and where a few rough situations led me to believe was the answer.

A couple of months after I turned 15 in May of 1994, maybe in July or so, David and I started drifting apart a little bit and we stopped hanging out as much. Really it was probably only about 3-4 weeks, but at that age, that amount of time seems like a lifetime, right? Anyway, this separation allowed him time to start hanging out with other guys in the neighborhood, and apparently, he started getting in a little bit of trouble with them – smoking weed, stealing, and shit like that. Soon after, his mother didn't allow him to hang out with me anymore. She blamed me for the trouble he was getting into. I tried to explain to her that I hadn't even been hanging out with him, and when he did whatever, he did to get in trouble, I was nowhere around – I had absolutely no involvement, didn't even know his other group of friends. And besides, he and I never got into any serious trouble when we were together; the biggest crime we did was smoke cigarettes on the platform that was right outside his bedroom window. She wasn't trying to hear it, though. Despite my attempt to explain, she continued to blame me for her son's problems.

A couple of months went by and I decided to call David to see if it was OK for him to hang out with me again. He told me it was, and to meet him at the park down the street from his house, a place where we'd often hung out together.

I was pretty happy to have my friend back, so I jumped on my dad's mountain bike and headed straight there, which was about 3 miles or so away. When I got there, I saw him, Dennis, Nicki, Darlene, and a couple of neighborhood kids who lived on their street.

When I rode up to where the group was I remained sitting on my bike – one foot on the pedal, one foot on the ground. I was excited to see my friends and thought that they'd be equally excited, but I quickly noticed a different energy from the group as they began to surround me. They started to accuse me of "talking shit," as they'd supposedly heard that I had been. I denied it of course, because it simply wasn't true.

The "talking shit" accusations went on for a couple of minutes, as did a few challenges to fight. I was sure I could whip each one individually, but I also knew I couldn't whip them as a group, which is how they were confronting me. Therefore, I did my best to avoid a physical fight from breaking out.

Eventually it turned out that another one of their grievances was that I had gotten a stain on one of Dennis's shirts, and that I'd better replace it. The shirt wasn't nothing but one of the 3-for-$10 T-shirts you get at the little Chinese fashion stores. It was a royal blue one, to be specific. My dad had the exact same shirt which he'd bought from the exact same place. I wore it all the time and I knew he didn't care much about it. So, upon me agreeing to replace Dennis's shirt, I rode my dad's bike all the way home, grabbed his shirt from wherever it was, rode my bike back to the park, gave them the shirt, then rode my dad's bike all the way back home again.

Never one to "steal" from my dad, the next day I told him the story of what had happened – about them surrounding me and me replacing Dennis's shirt with his. He couldn't care less about his cheap-ass T-shirt, but was pissed off they'd lured me into a setup where they surrounded and threatened me. He told me to "stay away from that family," that "they're all screwed up and nothing but trouble." I told my dad I wouldn't associate with them anymore. Though, to be honest, I was disappointed by the betrayal and the fact that it seemed I'd lost my friends – a family of sorts – for good. Nevertheless, this was the end of my friendship with David and I had no contact with him again until I got together with his sister in 1997. Now, 4 years later, David and I had completely different groups of friends and didn't like each other much. Despite this, we did our best to show each other a mutual respect.

$$\$\$\$\$\$$$

"David, what up?" I said as I stepped out of my car.

"What up, man; what's crackin'?" he replied back before taking a drag off his cigarette.

"Oh, you know, on my way to the studio. Had to stop by and get something to eat first, though, feel me? What are you 'bout to get into?"

"I'm about to get together with a few homies tonight, you know, to celebrate my birthday."

"Oh, shit, it's your birthday? Today?"

"Naw; tomorrow. But you know how that goes; I'ma kick it with the homies tonight, and tomorrow spend time with the family."

"Oh, OK. Well, happy birthday, homie," I said as I gave him daps.

"Thanks. So, yeah, we're just gonna get together, drink, smoke weed and shit, ya know?"

At the mention of "weed" I remembered the phone call I'd received earlier from my cousin. More for conversational purposes than really anything else, I told him about the information I'd learned a couple hours earlier.

"Yeah, yeah, I feel you. Hey, you know anyone who wants to hit a lick?" I asked.

"What kind of lick?"

"Well, my cousin called me up a couple of hours ago and said there's 75-100 Gs worth of weed growin' in a backyard in Fair Oaks. I guess it all just has to be cut and bagged. He asked me if I wanted to go get it, but said I'd need another person or two. I tried to get at Loki, but he wasn't home. I really ain't got nobody else to go, so if you and your homies wanna fuck with it, it's all good."

"Damn, 75-100 Gs?" he asked.

"Yeah; that's what he said. Kinda decent, huh?"

"Hell yeah. I don't know if anyone will wanna fuck with it, but I'll ask."

"OK, well, if you wanna do it, get at my cousin Kevin, he'll give you the details. You got his number?"

"Naw, I ain't got it."

"OK, here." I reached inside my briefcase full of pens, paper, A-DAT tapes, lyrics and studio notes, pulled out a pen and a piece of paper, wrote down Kevin's number and handed it to him.

$$$$$

See, David's known Kevin since back in the day, when we were friends. Kevin's a few years older than us and had a separate group of friends, ones who're closer to his age and into jackin' – car stereos, rims, and speakers mostly – but occasionally he'd hang out with us. At the time Kevin had a 1984 or 1985 Thunderbird with a phantom top and rocker panels, and it sat on 14-inch Roadstar spokes. He also had a Clarion CD player, Boston Acoustic mids and highs, and two Lanzar 12s in the trunk that used to shake the neighborhood. Being in it used to make me feel like I was the shit. The three of us used to roll around slammin' the "Above the Rim" soundtrack, which was new at the time. "Regulators" and

"Pour out a Little Liquor" were our favorite songs. Anyway, David and Kevin knew each other well, so I knew it was OK to tell David about the lick and give him Kevin's number.

$$$$$

"Hey, babe, your food's almost ready," my girlfriend said as she stuck her head out the door of the restaurant. Two-and-a-half sides of the restaurant has huge, glass windows. She must've seen me out there talking to David.

"OK, cool. Thank you."

"Hey, babe, come in here for a minute. I wanna talk to you," she said.

"A'ight," I told her. Then I told David I'd be back in a few minutes, after I hollered at his sister.

When I got inside the restaurant and walked up to where my girlfriend was, she stood up on her tiptoes and kissed me on the lips.

"Your food will be ready right now. I had 'em put extra chicken strips in there for you, too," she said. My girlfriend was the manager so she was able to compensate certain meals. One of the perks of her job is that I always ate for free. And ever since I was a kid I've loved Lyon's chicken strips and potato wedges with barbecue sauce.

"OK, thanks," I replied.

"Babe, I need you to do me a favor," she said.

I should've known there was going to be a catch to all this. "What's that?"

"I need you to take David by my mom's house so he can change, then drop him off at John's for me. If not, he's gonna have to wait till I get off work, and that's still several hours away. He doesn't wanna ask you himself, but would you do that for him, please?"

"I'll take him home, but I ain't tryna go to John's house. That's the opposite way from where I'm goin'."

John Fjelstad was David's best friend, and I didn't really care for David's crew. I didn't really care for David, either, but in the interest of my relationship with his sister I tried to be cordial. Occasionally I'd drop David off at John's house as a favor to his sister, but tonight, it really was the opposite way of my destination.

"Come on, babe. They're gonna get together to celebrate his birthday."

I did my best to come up with a solution – an alternative to me having to go out of my way; way out of my way. I only came up with one. I didn't like it much, but it was all I had.

"Look, let him use your car" – her car was really my car, but the one I let her use, which was a primer grey 1979 Grand Prix that I didn't care much about – "to go pick up John and take him to your mother's house until you get off work. That way they can kick it. When you get off work, they can drive here to pick you up, and from there you can take 'em wherever they wanna go."

"All right, that sounds OK," she said.

"But make sure he goes straight to John's house and back home until he has to pick you up. I don't want them driving around in my shit," I said as I gave her one of my serious looks – the kind that says "I ain't playin'."

"All right, I will. Let me get your food for you."

She went to the kitchen to get my food. Then she handed it to me and gave me another quick kiss on the lips.

"Have fun tonight, OK?" she said.

"I'll try," I said, a bit irritated that I felt sucked into a situation I really didn't like.

"I'll see you when you get home."

"OK."

I walked back out the restaurant towards my car, and when I got to David I gave him daps one more time, told him to have a happy birthday and that his sister wanted to talk to him, then jumped in my ride. I saw the look of disappointment on his face when he realized I wasn't giving him a ride to John's. He was unaware his sister and I had come up with an alternative plan.

$$$$$

I ate my food while driving to the studio. Brotha Lynch Hung's "Loaded" album was pounding out of my speakers. By the time I arrived at the studio my food was gone, I was full and ready for my session to start, which would be doing so in about an hour. I walked up to the front door and rang the buzzer.

"Who is it?" said the voice through the speaker.

"Kokain." My real name's Ron, but my friends call me Kokain because I'm white and I rhyme dope; get it?

"A'ight, I'll be right there."

Hitworks – the studio I was at – was located on Auburn Boulevard between Manzanita and Garfield, but closer to Garfield. It was in a cluster of industrial-type buildings across the street from "Showgirls," a strip club, next to a storage facility, and behind some other, small businesses. It wasn't actually on the street front, you had to drive in between the small businesses and storage facility in order to access the industrial building cluster in the back, one of which was the studio.

The door opened; it was Riq-Roq, the owner.

"What up, Kain?"

"What up, man; what's crackin' around here?" I asked as I walked into the building.

"Oh, you know, business as usual. I see you're early tonight."

"Yeah, ain't nothin' else crackin'. Thought I'd just come through and see who's here."

Hitworks was a studio created by Riq-Roq for artists who're trying to do something with hip-hop independently – artists who didn't have the backing of a record company, and therefore, didn't have the big bucks most music studios charged to use their facility. Instead of the usual $50-$75-an-hour rate that most places charged, Riq only charged $20 an hour. And if you bought a time block – paid for a decent-sized block of time upfront – the price would be even lower than that. For example, my cousin Kevin had purchased a block of 45 hours for $500, which brings the price down to something like … $11 and some change. And tonight, I was still using time from that 45-hour block.

Hitworks was also where a lot of people would hang out. Sometimes, even if one didn't have a session, they'd be there kickin' it, networking, whatever. And if you wanted to bring a friend or a couple of girls to kick it, that was all good, too – even if they had nothing to do with the production of hip-hop. That's just the kind of environment it was. It was a place to mingle. You had your regulars, but you also had your visitors, as well. So it wasn't unusual for me to be there an hour, or even several hours early.

$$$$$

Riq went back to the engineering room to tend to the ongoing session and I went to the kick-it room, which was actually the garage of the building. It had been converted into a little lounge with a couch, coffee table, soda machine, TV, Play Station, and a boom box. It was the only room where you could smoke and drink.

When I walked into the room there were two guys and a girl, sitting back, talking and smoking cigarettes. I didn't know them, so I introduced myself and then lit up a cigarette of my own. I'm a rather quiet guy, especially amongst people I am unfamiliar with, so while they continued their conversation, I remained quiet while doing my best to not seem standoffish.

After about 10 minutes or so of me being there, one of the guys (I can't remember his name) had decided he'd had enough of my silence.

"So what do you have going on tonight? Do you rap?"

"Yeah, I rap. I'm working on a CD, but tonight I just gotta dump a few beats," I said, assuming he knew what I was talking about.

"Dump a few beats?" he asked, obviously unsure of what I meant.

"Yeah. I gotta dump some beats we made, from my ASR-X Pro," I said as I pointed to my red beat machine, "to these A-DAT tapes. Each beat takes about an hour or so. I'm gonna dump four of 'em tonight; that way, when I'm ready to drop my vocals, I can just get down to business – without having to wait for each beat to be dumped in between."

"Oh, OK," he said. "I understand."

"Do you have any of your songs on you?" the girl asked curiously.

"Um… Yeah, I think I got a CD in my bag." Actually, I knew I had a CD in my bag but I wanted to act nonchalant. I reached in my bag, pulled out a burned CD and handed it to her.

"Can we listen to it?" she asked.

"Yeah, go 'head, I ain't trippin'."

The girl went to the boom box, opened the door to the CD player, put my CD in and pushed play. A few seconds later my song "Lyrical High" played through the speakers.

"Now you muthafuckas know that I be blowin' brains / 'Cause the shit that I spit is laced with cocain / Everybody knows I got my fans up in a trance / Throw my vocals in ya Vega, take it to the head and dance / Advance to another level in this game of the get you / If you fall off the train ain't nobody gonna miss you / Inhale my shit through the ears and trip too / I am Kokain, muthafucka, I'll rip you / A whole notha lung, to fill what I gotta say / Ha! Ha!, but anyway / I smoke a fat bleezy, smell the bomb on my shirt? / Take a hit off this potent shit and make ya lungs hurt / Now curtains get shifted, and skirts get lifted / My lyrical intoxication got the nation twisted / Lyrical high, Kain got the bomb, baby / There ain't no competition, so bring it on, baby...."

The three people in the room were bobbing their heads. I could tell they had underestimated me and were actually surprised and impressed by what they were hearing.

"That's you?" the girl asked.

"Yeah," I said as calm as I could, but really feeling excited that it seemed I was getting decent reviews.

"I like it," she said.

"Hell, yeah," said one of the guys. "This shit sounds tight."

"Thanks," I said.

We listened to the other two or three songs that were on the disc – Haters, Sabotage, and maybe one other, I can't really remember – and my crowd of three all agreed they'd buy the CD. That made me even happier, of course, since selling my CD was my ultimate goal.

We hung out a bit longer and I learned that they were there with their friend who was in the current session. Their friend was another guy I didn't know. However, while we were talking, three more guys showed up at the studio, two of whom I did know – G-Idez and Baby Regg. When they walked into the lounge room, I shook their hands while briefly introducing myself to the guy I didn't know. By now the energy level was rising a little bit and becoming a little more chaotic. G-Idez went to the back room, the engineering room, where Riq-Roq was working.

"What you finna do tonight; you got a session?" Regg asked as he gestured towards my equipment.

"Yeah, I gotta dump the beats we made for "Why," "Ain't No Competition," "Worst Nightmare," and "Back Up.""

Baby Regg knew what I was talking about. He was the one who'd been helping me produce my beats.

"Oh, OK. You ain't finna spit nothin' tonight?" he asked.

"Naw, I'ma just dump the beats."

"OK, well, next time you drop vocals bring me to the studio with you. I wanna help you with a few things. And if you need any verses from me, let me know and I got you," said Regg.

Regg was known in the local scene. He'd been around for a while and was once associated with Lynch. I was relatively new to recording, so I tried to get as much advice from him as possible. I respected his input, and to have him along was an honor.

"OK, fa sho'. I'm not sure when I'ma drop vocals next, but I'll be at you."

Regg lived right down the street from me and we kicked it together a few days out of the week. Unless I dropped my vocals the next day, it's likely we'd hang out before I did.

$$\$\$\$\$\$$$

The artist who'd been recording came into the lounge room and mentioned that his session was over. That meant it was my up-to-bat. It was around 10:20 or so; nothing's ever on time at the music studio. I grabbed my stuff and headed to the engineering room where Riq and G-Idez were at.

"What's on the agenda tonight?" Riq asked.

"I just wanna dump 3 or 4 beats."

"All right. You got all your shit?"

"Yeah." I began to hook up my ASR-X Pro and upload the first beat.

$$\$\$\$\$\$$$

Dumping beats is a simple, but long and boring process. See, each individual sound you hear in a beat – the drum kick, the snare, the high-hats, the bassline, the strings, whatever – has to be dumped onto an A-DAT (at least at this time, now it's mostly all done via computer) one sound at a time, each on an individual track of its own. This way, you can tweak each sound/instrument individually. Typically, you'll dump each sound/instrument for around five minutes to ensure you have enough for your three- to four-minute song.

$$$$$

Around three hours had went by, a few people had come and went, and it was somewhere in the area of 1:20 AM when we – me, Riq, and some guy I didn't know – heard the buzzer ring, making us aware someone was at the door wanting to come in.

"Who is it?" Riq asked into a mic that allowed him to communicate from the engineering room through the speaker outside.

"Loki."

"Loki?" Riq asked as he looked back at me and the other guy in a way that questioned if either of us knew who Loki was.

"Loki's my boy, he's here for me. He's Kilo's brother," I told Riq. "I'll go get him."

Riq had never met Loki before, as the only other time Loki had been to the studio was with me, and he waited in the car while I dropped something off. However, Loki's brother, Kilo, frequented the studio pretty often and Riq was well aware of who Kilo was.

I walked to the front door to let Loki in.

"Loki, what up, man?" I said as I opened the front door and he stepped into the building, giving me daps.

"Shit, I got your message. Everything all good?" he asked sounding a bit concerned.

"Yeah, yeah, everything's all right."

"I got your message and it seemed kind of urgent."

I admit, I made it seem kind of urgent to increase my odds of getting a response. See, Loki did not like to come to the studio – which is why he'd only been there once before and stayed in the car.

"Naw, naw, naw. My cousins got a come-up and he's urgent about getting it done. He called me earlier to see if I wanted to do it but said I'd need one or two more people. I called you to see if you wanted to do it with me and you didn't answer, so I went by your place to see if you were there but you weren't. That's when I left the note."

"Oh, yeah, I was at work," Loki replied. Loki had some nighttime janitorial job and could basically come and go as he pleased as long as the work got done.

"What kind of come-up?" Loki asked a bit skeptically, as he wasn't really into anything too crazy.

"Hold on," I said.

I went to let Riq know I was going to smoke a cigarette and that I'd be back in a few minutes. Once Loki and I were outside I told him the details.

"Well, according to Kevin," I said as I lit my cigarette, "there's a house in Fair Oaks with about 75-100 Gs worth of weed growing in the backyard. Supposedly there ain't nobody home right now and all we gotta do is hop the fence, cut it down, and be off. What do you think?"

"Man; it sounds tempting. 75-100 Gs and nobody's home?" he asked.

"That's what Kevin's saying. I guess somebody tried to get it earlier and ended up beating on somebody who lives there with a bat. Kevin says they're all at the hospital and the weed's still in the back yard."

"Damn, bro, somebody already tried to get it?"

"Yeah. Earlier today."

"Man...it might not be a good idea to go back tonight. They might be on it, ya know? They might be waiting."

"I know. And I ain't even gonna lie, I ain't tryna go up in nobody's back yard without a vest. If somebody went up in my yard tryna steal my bushes, I'm dumpin'."

"Hell yeah I'm dumpin," Loki agreed as we both chuckled.

Loki had a bulletproof vest. I figured if I was going to go up in somebody's yard, I'd want to wear it. Of course, he'd want to wear it too, but that's something we'd have to figure out later.

I didn't smoke weed. In fact, I didn't use any drugs – not even alcohol. And I didn't sell weed, either; I sold cocaine. But my boy Loki was a real weedhead, and I could see the gears in his mind turning. He was calculating shit; weighing out the pros and cons.

"Naw, man; I just got off work and I'm fuckin' tired. We'd have to go all the way to my house, then get at Kevin for the details, then smash up to wherever in Fair Oaks... I think it's too late. By the time we get there it'll be 3:00 AM and I'm already runnin' on fumes."

"Yeah, I feel you. I'm pretty tired too," I said.

I was. Unless I was at the studio, most nights I'd be asleep by 10:00 PM.

"You still commin' through tomorrow, though, to make some beats, right?"

"Yeah, fa sho. I'll be there as soon as I wake up and shower," I assured him.

"Well, maybe when we get together tomorrow we'll slide by and check it out, see if it's doable," he suggested.

"Yeah, if Kevin will give us the directions to the place. I think a few people are plottin' on it so he's tryna keep the location close to the vest. We'll try, though."

The idea sounded good to me. It's better to be safe than sorry, and it's never a good idea to go into something like this blind.

"Well, what're you gonna do right now?" I asked.

"I'ma take my black-ass home and go to sleep."

"Why don't you come kick it in the back for a minute? My session's almost up, ain't nobody you know here."

"Man, you know I ain't tryna get caught up in no bullshit," he said.

$$$$$

See, Loki wasn't into gangbanging, but his brother Kilo was. And a few years prior to this, while Loki and Kilo were at a car audio shop on Arden Boulevard, a rival gang member had pulled a gun out on them. In return, Kilo pulled out his gun – a 357 – and plugged the guy three times, killing him. Before taking off, however, they grabbed the guy's gun off the ground. They consulted the family attorney on the matter and he convinced Kilo to turn himself in and surrender the dead guy's gun. He did, and after 18 months of fighting the case he was given a deal and released on time served. It was clearly self-defense. However, members of the dead guy's gang wanted to retaliate by killing Kilo and Loki. Because of this, Loki didn't like being anywhere where he might get into a situation, a place one of them might show up at, thus; he wasn't trying to hang around a hip-hop studio where a lot of people went in and out of. Now, I wouldn't say Loki's scary, but he's extremely cautious and careful.

$$$$$

"Naw, bro, I know. You'll be straight. Ain't nobody around here," I assured him.

We walked to the engineering room where Riq was dumping my beat and I introduced him to Loki.

"Riq-Roq, this is Loki, Kilo's older brother; Loki, this is Riq-Roq."

"Hey, Riq, what's up, man?" Loki said as he extended his fist towards Riq to receive daps.

"Hey, Loki, how you doin'?" Riq responded as he extended his fist to dap Loki's. "So Kilo's your brother, huh?"

218

"Yeah," said Loki.

"OK, OK. So what you guys got goin' on tonight?" Riq asked as he turned back towards the mixing board to tend to business.

"Shit," I said. "We're gonna finish up this last beat and be out – call it a night."

"Yeah," Riq replied, "it's getting pretty late." It was around 1:45 AM.

$$\$\$\$\$\$$$

We finished up dumping the last beat I had planned for the night, then I gave Riq my log sheet to sign off the hours. See, when you buy a block, Riq provides you with a log sheet stating the amount of time you purchased. It also has individual sections for you to write the date and time you used the studio, what you worked on, as well as a place for both the artist's and Riq's signatures verifying that the time was used. It helps Riq keep track of how much time he owes you, and it helps you keep track of how much time you have left before you have to come out the pocket for more.

In the parking lot of the studio, Loki and I gave daps, confirmed we'd get together the next morning, then drove off toward our apartments; mine is on the way to his.

$$\$\$\$\$\$$$

As I pulled into the gates of my apartment, I felt relieved to be home. It had been a rather long night and I was looking forward to getting in my bed and going to sleep. However, when I pulled around back to where my apartment was located, something seemed wrong. It took about half a second before I realized what it was. My other car was gone, which meant my girlfriend was not home. Where the fuck could she be?

Once I pulled into my parking space and got out, I noticed the light from the TV flashing in our bedroom window. This meant she must've been home, then went back out. *Hmm*, I thought. Then I remembered it was her brother's birthday and figured she was either out with him, giving him a ride somewhere, or picking him up. Shit, she might even be at her mom's.

I gathered up my equipment, unlocked the front door and went inside. My arms were full, so I shut the door with my foot and didn't bother to lock it right away like I usually do. I set my stuff down on the table we had set up in our dining room, and then walked to our bedroom to kick off my shoes and empty all the things from my pockets onto my-side-of-the-bed's end table. When I walked into my room, I was startled by a surprise; my girlfriend was lying in bed, watching TV.

"Oh, shit, you're home?" I asked.

"Yeah, I got home about an hour ago," she replied. It was then that I became extremely irritated.

"Well, if you're home, where the fuck is my car?"

"David's got it."

"Why the fuck does David got it?"

"'Cause he needed transportation and I didn't think you'd mind," she said as innocently as she could. She knew she'd fucked up.

"What do you mean you didn't think I'd mind?! Of course I mind! I don't want him out there runnin' around in my shit! What the fuck are you thinking?!"

"Calm down. It's his birthday and he needed transportation. You said he could use it to go pick up John, what's the difference?"

I was pissed. I try to do something nice for someone, someone I don't even like, and this is my reward?

"I was very clear that he was to pick up John and go straight home until you got off work. Period."

"Well, he called me and said he needed to do a few other things so I told him to go ahead. I got a ride home from my friend. Everything will be OK. Stop trippin'," she said defensively.

"Man, I don't even like your brother; or his little bitch-ass friends. The only reason I don't beat his ass is because of you. If it wasn't for that, I'd teach him how to respect somebody."

On top of the bad blood from 1994, her brother had also said some things about me behind my back while I was in CYA; he and his best friend at the time, Marcus. He didn't know I knew, but I did. The only reason why I didn't give him one of those good old-fashioned ass kickin's is because I didn't want to deal with the drama that was sure to come afterwards; especially with his bipolar mother.

"Respect, respect, respect; that's all you talk about. Quit trippin'," she said.

At that moment, I heard my front door open. Not knowing who was invading my home, it startled the shit out of me. I stepped out of my bedroom to see what the hell was going on; it was David and John, barging into my spot. Once again, a huge form of disrespect. I was about to explode into a rage on these two disrespectful dirt-bags, but seeing the look of panic on their faces distracted me from my rage.

"It's all bad," David said.

"What do you mean it's all bad?" I asked.

"It's all bad, fool," David repeated.

"What's going on out there?" asked my girlfriend from the bedroom.

"Mind your own fuckin' business," I responded, still pissed off at her.

"We need you to give us a ride home," David said. "We need to get home."

I wasn't sure what was going on, but the look of panic on David and John's faces were convincing and outweighed my lack of desire to drive anywhere. "OK, I'll take you guys home," I said.

"What are you guys doing?" asked my girlfriend in an irritating, complaining-type tone as she came out the bedroom and saw David and John in our living room.

"Nothing," I said. "Go to bed and mind your own fuckin' business."

Me, David and John got in my car and I began to drive out of my apartment complex.

"Where you guys going, your mom's or John's?" I asked, as the two places were in opposite directions.

"Take me to my girl's," David replied, referring to his girlfriend Cynthia who lived about two miles or so from my apartment.

"Take me home," John said. John's house was in the same direction as Cynthia's, but just a little further.

"So, what's going on, man, you guys straight?" I asked, feeling a weird energy inside of my car.

"Naw, it's all bad, fool," David said again.

"Yeah, it's all bad, man," John confirmed.

I began to worry about what could've happened. About a year prior to this, John and their other best friend, Marcus, the guy who'd been talking shit about me along with David while I was in CYA, had caught a murder beef. They'd seen two brothers, both of whom were from a rival gang, and Marcus shot one in the head, blowing his brains out, then shot the other several times, but without killing him. Marcus went on the run and then ended up killing himself around three months later. John was arrested but let out on bail, since Marcus was the shooter and now dead. Anyway, this incident caused the neighborhood to be a bit funky, if you know what I mean. And I started to wonder if maybe they did something in my car that would now make my car and whoever's in it – mostly me, my girlfriend, and her 4-year-old son – a target. I started to get irritated again. I *told* her I didn't want nobody driving around in my shit!

It only took about three minutes to get to David's girlfriend's house. Once we got there he got out, and without saying a word to John or I, went to her front door. When it opened, he went in and I drove off.

John and I arrived at his house about a minute after that. The drive over there was a bit awkward, as we had no connection with each other other than David, which was already an awkward situation within itself. When he stepped out of my car he said, "OK, thanks, fool," and that was that.

On my drive home I still felt a weird energy inside of my car. I wasn't sure what was going on, but I admit I was curious. When I walked inside my apartment, there was my girlfriend, looking at me as if she had a right to be angry.

"What did you guys do?" she asked.

"Nothing; I took 'em home; don't fuckin' worry about it," I said, still angry with her.

I took off my clothes, washed up a bit, and then jumped into bed next to my girlfriend. We went to sleep without saying another word to each other.

$$\$\$\$\$\$$$

Conspiracy Theory, Mike Enemigo, available now on thecellblock.net and Amazon, or by sending $12 plus $5 S/H to: The Cell Block; PO Box 1025; Racho Cordova, CA 95741

THE CELL BLOCK

BOOK SUMMARIES

MIKE ENEMIGO is the new prison/street art sensation who has written and published several books. He is inspired by emotion; hope; pain; dreams and nightmares. He physically lives somewhere in a California prison cell where he works relentlessly creating his next piece. His mind and soul are elsewhere; seeing, studying, learning, and drawing inspiration to tear down suppressive walls and inspire the culture by pushing artistic boundaries.

THE CELL BLOCK is an independent multimedia company with the objective of accurately conveying the prison/street experience with the credibility and honesty that only one who has lived it can deliver, through literature and other arts, and to entertain and enlighten while doing so. Everything published by The Cell Block has been created by a prisoner, while in a prison cell.

THE BEST RESOURCE DIRECTORY FOR PRISONERS, $17.95 & $5.00 S/H: This book has over 1,450 resources for prisoners! Includes: Pen-Pal Companies! Non-Nude Photo Sellers! Free Books and Other Publications! Legal Assistance! Prisoner Advocates! Prisoner Assistants! Correspondence Education! Money-Making Opportunities! Resources for Prison Writers, Poets, Artists! And much, much more! Anything you can think of doing from your prison cell, this book contains the resources to do it!

A GUIDE TO RELAPSE PREVENTION FOR PRISONERS, $15.00 & $5.00 S//H: This book provides the information and guidance that can make a real difference in the preparation of a comprehensive relapse prevention plan. Discover how to meet the parole board's expectation using these proven and practical principles. Included is a blank template and sample relapse prevention plan to assist in your preparation.

CONSPIRACY THEORY, $12.00 & $4.00 S/H: Kokain is an upcoming rapper trying to make a name for himself in the Sacramento, CA underground scene, and Nicki is his girlfriend. One night, in October, Nicki's brother, along with her brother's best friend, go to rob a house of its $100,000 marijuana crop. It goes wrong; shots are fired and a man is killed. Later, as investigators begin closing in on Nicki's brother and his friend, they, along with the help of a few others, create a way to make Kokain take the fall .... The conspiracy begins.

THEE ENEMY OF THE STATE (SPECIAL EDITION), $9.99 & $4.00 S/H: Experience the inspirational journey of a kid who was introduced to the art of rapping in 1993, struggled between his dream of becoming a professional rapper and the reality of the streets, and was finally offered a recording deal in 1999, only to be arrested minutes later and eventually sentenced to life in prison for murder... However, despite his harsh reality, he dedicated himself to hip-hop once again, and with resilience and determination, he sets out to prove he may just be one of the dopest rhyme writers/spitters ever .... At this point, it becomes deeper than rap .... Welcome to a preview of the greatest story you never heard.

LOST ANGELS: $15.00 & $5.00: David Rodrigo was a child who belonged to no world; rejected for his mixed heritage by most of his family and raised by an outcast uncle in the mean streets of East L.A. Chance cast him into a far darker and more devious pit of intrigue that stretched from the barest gutters to the halls of power in the great city. Now, to survive the clash of lethal forces arrayed about him, and to protect those he loves, he has only two allies; his quick wits, and the flashing blade that earned young David the street name, Viper.

LOYALTY AND BETRAYAL DELUXE EDITION, $19.99 & $7.00 S/H: Chunky was an associate of and soldier for the notorious Mexican Mafia – La Eme. That is, of course, until he was betrayed by those he was most loyal to. Then he vowed to become their worst enemy. And though they've attempted to kill him numerous times, he still to this day is running around making a mockery of their organization .... This is the story of how it all began.

MONEY IZ THE MOTIVE: SPECIAL 2-IN-1 EDITION, $19.99 & $7.00 S/H: Like most kids growing up in the hood, Kano has a dream of going from rags to riches. But when his plan to get fast money by robbing the local "mom and pop" shop goes wrong, he quickly finds himself sentenced to serious prison time. Follow Kano as he is schooled to the ways of the game by some of the most respected OGs whoever did it; then is set free and given the resources to put his schooling into action and build the ultimate hood empire...

DEVILS & DEMONS, $15.00 & $5.00 S/H: When Talton leaves the West Coast to set up shop in Florida he meets the female version of himself: A drug dealing murderess with psychological issues. A whirlwind of sex, money and murder inevitably ensues and Talton finds himself on the run from the law with nowhere to turn to. When his team from home finds out he's in trouble, they get on a plane heading south...

THE ART & POWER OF LETTER WRITING FOR PRISONERS: DELUXE EDITION $19.99 & $7.00 S/H: When locked inside a prison cell, being able to write well is the most powerful skill you can have! Learn how to increase your power by writing high-quality personal and formal letters! Includes letter templates, pen-pal website strategies, punctuation guide and more!

THE PRISON MANUAL: $24.99 & $7.00 S/H: The Prison Manual is your all-in-one book on how to not only survive the rough terrain of the American prison system, but use it to your advantage so you can THRIVE from it! How to Use Your Prison Time to YOUR Advantage; How to Write Letters that Will Give You Maximum Effectiveness; Workout and Physical Health Secrets that Will Keep You as FIT as Possible; The Psychological impact of incarceration and How to Maintain Your MAXIMUM Level of Mental Health; Prison Art Techniques; Fulfilling Food Recipes; Parole Preparation Strategies and much, MUCH more!

GET OUT, STAY OUT!, $16.95 & $5.00 S/H: This book should be in the hands of everyone in a prison cell.

It reveals a challenging but clear course for overcoming the obstacles that stand between prisoners and their freedom. For those behind bars, one goal outshines all others: GETTING OUT! After being released, that goal then shifts to STAYING OUT! This book will help prisoners do both. It has been masterfully constructed into five parts that will help prisoners maximize focus while they strive to accomplish whichever goal is at hand.

MOB$TAR MONEY, $12.00 & $4.00 S/H: After Trey's mother is sent to prison for 75 years to life, he and his little brother are moved from their home in Sacramento, California, to his grandmother's house in Stockton, California where he is forced to find his way in life and become a man on his own in the city's grimy streets. One day, on his way home from the local corner store, Trey has a rough encounter with the neighborhood bully. Luckily, that's when Tyson, a member of the MOBTAR, a local "get money" gang comes to his aid. The two kids quickly become friends, and it doesn't take long before Trey is embraced into the notorious MOB$TAR money gang, which opens the door to an adventure full of sex, money, murder and mayhem that will change his life forever... You will never guess how this story ends!

BLOCK MONEY, $12.00 & $4.00 S/H: Beast, a young thug from the grimy streets of central Stockton, California lives The Block; breathes The Block; and has committed himself to bleed The Block for all it's worth until his very last breath. Then, one day, he meets Nadia; a stripper at the local club who piques his curiosity with her beauty, quick-witted intellect and rider qualities. The problem? She has a man – Esco – a local kingpin with money and power. It doesn't take long, however, before a devious plot is hatched to pull off a heist worth an indeterminable amount of money. Following the acts of treachery, deception and betrayal are twists and turns and a bloody war that will leave you speechless!

HOW TO HUSTLE AND WIN: SEX, MONEY, MURDER EDITION $15.00 & $5.00 S/H: How To Hu$tle and Win: Sex, Money, Murder edition is the grittiest, underground self-help manual for the 21st century street entrepreneur in print. Never has there been such a book written for today's gangsters, goons and go-getters. This self-help handbook is an absolute must-have for anyone who is actively connected to the streets.

RAW LAW: Your Rights, & How to Sue When They are Violated! $15.00 & $5.00 S/H: Raw Law For Prisoners is a clear and concise guide for prisoners and their advocates to understanding civil rights laws guaranteed to prisoners under the US Constitution, and how to successfully file a lawsuit when those rights have been violated! From initial complaint to trial, this book will take you through the entire process, step by step, in simple, easy-to-understand terms. Also included are several examples where prisoners have sued prison officials successfully, resulting in changes of unjust rules and regulations and recourse for rights violations, oftentimes resulting in rewards of thousands, even millions of dollars in damages! If you feel your rights have been violated, don't lash out at guards, which is usually ineffective and only makes matters worse. Instead, defend yourself successfully by using the legal system, and getting the power of the courts on your side!

HOW TO WRITE URBAN BOOKS FOR MONEY & FAME: $16.95 & $5.00 S/H: Inside this book you will learn the true story of how Mike Enemigo and King Guru have received money and fame from inside their prison cells by writing urban books; the secrets to writing hood classics so you, too, can be caked up and famous; proper punctuation using hood examples; and resources you can use to achieve your money motivated ambitions! If you're a prisoner who want to write urban novels for money and fame, this must-have manual will give you all the game!

PRETTY GIRLS LOVE BAD BOYS: An Inmate's Guide to Getting Girls: $15.00 & $5.00 S/H: Tired of the same, boring, cliché pen pal books that don't tell you what you really need to know? If so, this book is for you! Anything you need to know on the art of long and short distance seduction is included within these pages! Not only does it give you the science of attracting pen pals from websites, it also includes psychological profiles and instructions on how to seduce any woman you set your sights on! Includes interviews of women who have fallen in love with prisoners, bios for pen pal ads, pre-written love letters, romantic poems, love-song lyrics, jokes and much, much more! This book is the ultimate guide – a must-have for any prisoner who refuses to let prison walls affect their MAC'n.

THE LADIES WHO LOVE PRISONERS, $15.00 & $5.00 S/H: New Special Report reveals the secrets of real women who have fallen in love with prisoners, regardless of crime, sentence, or location. This info will give you a HUGE advantage in getting girls from prison.

GET OUT, GET RICH: HOW TO GET PAID LEGALLY WHEN YOU GET OUT OF PRISON!, $16.95 & $5.00 S/H: Many of you are incarcerated for a money-motivated crime. But w/ today's tech & opportunities, not only is the crime-for-money risk/reward ratio not strategically wise, it's not even necessary. You can earn much more money by partaking in anyone of the easy, legal hustles explained in this book, regardless of your record. Help yourself earn an honest income so you can not only make a lot of money, but say good-bye to penitentiary chances and prison forever! (Note: Many things in this book can even he done from inside prison.) (ALSO PUBLISHED AS HOOD MILLIONAIRE: HOW TO HUSTLE AND WIN LEGALLY!)

THE MILLIONAIRE PRISONER: SPECIAL 2-IN-1 EDITION $24.99 & $7.00 S/H: Why wait until you get out of prison to achieve your dreams? Here's a blueprint that you can use to become successful! The Millionaire Prisoner is your complete reference to overcoming any obstacle in prison. You won't be able to put it down! With this book you will discover the secrets to: Making money from your cell! Obtain FREE money for correspondence courses! Become an expert on any topic! Develop the habits of the rich! Network with celebrities! Set up your own website! Market your products, ideas and services! Successfully use prison pen pal websites! All of this and much, much more! This book has enabled thousands of prisoners to succeed and it will show you the way also!

THE CEO MANUAL: HOW TO START A BUSINESS WHEN YOU GET OUT OF PRISON,

$16.95 & $5.00 S/H: $16.95 & $5 S/H: This new book will teach you the simplest way to start your own business when you get out of prison. Includes: Start-up Steps! The Secrets to Pulling Money from Investors! How to Manage People Effectively! How To Legally Protect Your Assets from "them"! Hundreds of resources to get you started, including a list of 'loan friendly" banks! (ALSO PUBLISHED AS CEO MANUAL: START A BUSINESS, BE A BOSS!)

THE MONEY MANUAL: UNDERGROUND CASH SECRETS EXPOSED! 16.95 & $5.00 S/H: Becoming a millionaire is equal parts what you make, and what you don't spend-- AKA save. All Millionaires and Billionaires have mastered the art of not only making money, but keeping the money they make (remember Donald Trump's tax maneuvers?), as well as establishing credit so that they are loaned money by banks and trusted with money from investors: AKA OPM -- other people's money. And did you know there are millionaires and billionaires just waiting to GIVE money away? It's true! These are all very-little known secrets 'they" don't want YOU to know about, but that I'm exposing in my new book!

OJ'S LIFE BEHIND BARS, $15.00 & $5 S/H: In 1994, Heisman Trophy winner and NFL superstar OJ Simpson was arrested for the brutal murder of his ex-wife Nicole Brown-Simpson and her friend Ron Goldman. In 1995, after the "trial of the century," he was acquitted of both murders, though most of the world believes he did it. In 2007 OJ was again arrested, but this time in Las Vegas, for armed robbery and kidnapping. On October 3, 2008 he was found guilty sentenced to 33 years and was sent to Lovelock Correctional Facility, in Lovelock, Nevada. There he met inmate-author Vernon Nelson. Vernon was granted a true, insider's perspective into the mind and life of one of the country's most notorious men; one that has never provided...until now.

KITTY KAT, ADULT ENTERTAINMENT RESOURCE BOOK, $24.99 & $7.00 S/H: This book is jam packed with hundreds of sexy non nude photos including photo spreads. The book contains the complete info on sexy photo sellers, hot magazines, page turning bookstore, sections on strip clubs, porn stars, alluring models, thought provoking stories and must see movies.

PRISON LEGAL GUIDE, $24.99 & $7.00 S/H: The laws of the U.S. Judicial system are complex, complicated, and always growing and changing. Many prisoners spend days on end digging through its intricacies. Pile on top of the legal code the rules and regulations of a correctional facility, and you can see how high the deck is being stacked against you. Correct legal information is the key to your survival when you have run afoul of the system (or it is running afoul of you). Whether you are an accomplished jailhouse lawyer helping newbies learn the ropes, an old head fighting bare-knuckle for your rights in the courts, or a hustler just looking to beat the latest write-up – this book has something for you!

PRISON HEALTH HANDBOOK, $19.99 & $7.00 S/H: The Prison Health Handbook is your one-stop go-to source for information on how to maintain your best health while inside the American prison system. Filled with information, tips, and secrets from doctors, gurus, and other experts, this book will educate you on such things as proper workout and exercise regimens; yoga benefits for prisoners; how to meditate effectively; pain management tips; sensible dieting solutions; nutritional knowledge; an understanding of various cancers, diabetes, hepatitis, and other diseases all too common in prison; how to effectively deal with mental health issues such as stress, PTSD, anxiety, and depression; a list of things your doctors DON'T want YOU to know; and much, much more!

All books are available at thecellblock.net and Amazon. Prices may differ between Amazon and our website.

You can also order by sending a money order or institutional check to:

The Cell Block
PO Box 1025
Rancho Cordova, CA 95741

Made in the USA
Monee, IL
31 July 2021